# SAVING CHARLOTTE

## ELIZABETH KELLY

EK PUBLISHING INC.

# SAVING CHARLOTTE

**Two worlds collide.**

Charlotte Montgomery's shattered world has left her reeling.

Now, a drug dealing motorcycle club has taken her and the salon hostage.

She's too numb to care until her friend's life is threatened. To save him, she'll play a dangerous game with the rough and sexy club member, Ren. A game that will forever change her.

The last thing Ren wants is a hostage situation.

But when the club president shoots a cop and takes him and a salon full of stylists hostage, Ren's powerless to stop it. Getting himself and his fellow club members out of this mess is his top priority. However, his immediate attraction to Charlotte is an unwelcome and potentially killer distraction.

Drug fueled, the increasingly unstable club president demands Ren play by club rules or watch Charlotte die. Ren has no choice but to obey.

Will Charlotte and Ren's mutual attraction be the key to saving them both, or the complication that gets them killed?

# CHAPTER 1

"How are Melody and the kids?" Charlotte turned the clippers on and carefully shaved the back of Vince's neck.

"They're good - real good." Vince smiled at her in the mirror as she finished shaving his neck, brushing away the small bits of hair that still clung to his sunburned neck. "Jade's leaving for college next week."

Charlotte shook her head in disbelief. "I can't believe she's starting college this year."

"You and me both." Vince grimaced. "And why she feels the need to move halfway across the country is beyond me."

"Mel is going to miss her," Charlotte said.

"Yeah, she really will," Vince said.

"At least you still have Daniel at home."

"True," Vince said. "Although this is his last year of high school, and I imagine he'll choose a college as far away from here as he can."

"This is a small place. Kids are always eager to leave."

"Yeah, but I had hoped that one of them might follow their old man's career path."

Charlotte smiled at him. "Jade is going into criminology."

"Yeah, but it ain't the same as being a cop. We both know she'll become a lawyer like her mother. And Daniel is planning on majoring in theatre. Theatre! Tell me, what kind of job will the kid get from that?"

Before Charlotte could reply, Vince said, "Mel says kids need to follow their own path, and we need to encourage Daniel to follow his dreams. I don't disagree, but we'll see how she feels when Danny's thirty-eight and living in our basement."

Charlotte laughed, and Vince grinned at her in the mirror. "It's good to hear you laugh, Charlotte. Mel and I have been worried about you."

"I'm fine, Vince."

He grunted and shifted in the chair before glancing around the salon. The other two hair stylists were chatting in the back of the salon, and Darlene, the receptionist, was on the phone booking an appointment.

"I doubt you're fine," he said. "It's only been three months."

"True." Charlotte swept the bits of iron-grey hair from his cape-covered shoulders. "But he was sick for nearly two years before that. It gives a person time to prepare."

"I know." He drew his hand free from the cape and placed it on top of hers. "It doesn't mean you're not lonely, though."

"No, it doesn't," Charlotte said. "But there's relief in knowing he isn't suffering anymore."

She squeezed Vince's hand briefly before unbuttoning the cape and carefully shaking it out. "Are you heading home now?"

He shook his head. "Nah. I'm working late tonight. We've been having some trouble with a motorcycle gang that showed up a couple of months ago. We suspect they've been trafficking and dealing in drugs. As if we don't have enough trouble with that already."

He eased his body out of the chair and straightened his uniform before placing his police cap back on his head. Charlotte followed him to the reception, leaning against the counter as Vince paid Darlene. As usual, he left her a generous tip, and she smiled in thanks at him.

"Why don't you come by this weekend? I know Mel would love to see you again." Vince slid his wallet into his back pocket.

"That sounds nice. Tell Mel to text me," Charlotte said.

Vince hugged her hard. "You know if you need anything, anything at all, you can just call us, right?"

"I know, Vince. Thank you."

He left the salon as Charlotte returned to her station to sweep up the bits of hair on the floor around her chair. Her back hurt, and she had the beginning of a headache, but she thought she had done an admirable job of convincing Vince that she was fine.

It wasn't that she wasn't fine, she decided. She wasn't anything. She felt no overwhelming sadness or loneliness, nor did she feel happiness or joy. The morning after Rick died, she woke to discover a curious sort of numbness had swallowed her every emotion as neatly as the whale had swallowed Jonah.

She'd hidden it well from her friends and family. Only her therapist knew about her sudden inability to feel anything at all. She didn't believe she was suicidal, but she also couldn't deny that the thought of her own death brought only a weary kind of relief.

She swallowed hard, trying to force herself into feeling some kind of terror or even discomfort at the idea of her very existence fading out like a dying candle, but there was only the numbness. She swept up some hair that had migrated under her station. There was no point in forcing herself to feel something she didn't. She had to work through the grief just like her therapist kept telling her. This lack of emotion, this numbness, was just a cleverly masqueraded stage of grief – it would pass eventually.

Her head swivelled toward the salon's front door as the loud pop of firecrackers came from outside. She wandered to reception as Darlene stood up from behind her desk. "Did you hear that?"

Charlotte nodded. "Weird to have firecrackers this time of the year."

"I don't think it was firecrackers." Darlene hesitated. "It sounded like gunfire to me. Maybe you shouldn't go out there, Charlotte."

Charlotte, who was pushing open the front door, glanced over her shoulder at the young woman. "I'm just going to check -"

Vince staggered through the open door, his face pale and his hand pressed against his side.

"Charlotte, lock the door," he wheezed. He toppled over, knocking her off her feet. She gasped with pain as she fell to the floor, her elbow slamming painfully into the hard tile. With a grunt of effort, she pushed Vince off of her and onto his back as Rita and Helen hurried over from the back of the salon.

"Vince?" She stared in disbelief at the bright bloom of blood seeping through the front of Vince's shirt.

"Charlotte," he groaned, "the door – quick."

Before she could climb to her feet, the bell over the door rang out, and three men entered the salon. All three were dressed similarly in dirty jeans, white t-shirts and leather vests. The first man had a gun in his hand, and Vince's gun was shoved into the front of his pants. He pointed the gun in his hand at Darlene.

"Lock the door - now."

She stared frozen at him, and he slapped her across the head. "Now, bitch!"

She stumbled to the door and locked it as the second man pulled the shade down over the large picture window. He moved to the door, shoving Darlene out of the way and turning the open sign to close before pulling the shade on the door.

The third man, he was tall and broad with long dark hair tied back in a ponytail and a thick beard covering his face, grabbed a stack of towels from Rita's station and knelt beside Vince. He pressed two of the towels to the gunshot on Vince's side and grabbed Charlotte's hand.

"Apply pressure," he growled to her, pressing her hand down hard on the towels. She did as he asked as he leaned over Vince and felt for the pulse in his neck.

"Hang on, old man," he breathed.

Charlotte looked at Vince. He was staring at the man above him, and Charlotte could have sworn that a flicker of recognition crossed Vince's face.

"What the fuck are you doing, Ren? Leave him!" the first man snapped.

The man named Ren stared at Charlotte for a moment, his dark grey eyes assessing her coolly. "Don't let up on the pressure. Do you hear me?"

She nodded as he stood and returned to the other two men.

"What the hell, Ren? Who gives a shit about that old fart?"

Ren glared at the smaller man. "Do you want to add murder to your list of crimes, Steve? Killing a cop will get you the chair, you moron."

"Fuck you, Ren!" Steve spat. Like Ren, his dirty blonde

hair was long and tied back in a ponytail. His stocky body was nearly vibrating with excitement, and his faded blue eyes were darting back and forth. Charlotte suspected he was high on something as he turned and shoved Darlene toward Rita and Helen. The three women huddled together as the second man paced back and forth at the door.

"Jesus Christ," he moaned. He had a blue bandana on his head, and he swiped it off to reveal a bald and gleaming skull and then wiped the sweat from his face with the bandana. "We're dead, man. We're so fucking dead."

"We're fine, Jasper," Steve grunted.

"Are you kidding me?" Jasper was the smallest of the three. Short and thin, his jeans hanging from his non-existent ass and his leather vest wrapped loosely around his chest, he looked like he was going to vomit. "You shot a goddamn cop! Ren's right – we're going to fry for this."

Steve slammed his fist down on the reception desk. "It's not like I had much choice. Stupid fucking pig practically fell onto our deal."

Ren moved the shade and peered out. "We have to go. Staying here is dangerous."

"Where the hell are we gonna go?" Steve said.

"We grab our bikes and ride," Ren said. "For Christ's sake, three different people watched us chase that bleeding cop in here. This place is going to be crawling with cops at any moment."

As if his words summoned them, the faint sound of sirens could be heard.

"Shit!" Ren dropped the shade and stared at Jasper. "Go check the back door. Make sure it's locked."

Jasper disappeared into the back of the salon as Charlotte took Vince's hand.

Ren knelt beside her again and pulled the belt from Vince's pants. He slid it under Vince, and Vince groaned with pain. Ren pushed Charlotte's hand out of the way before adding more towels to the blood-soaked ones. He buckled the belt so that it held the towels against Vince's bleeding side.

Charlotte leaned over him. "Vince? Can you hear me? Squeeze my hand."

Vince squeezed her hand with surprising strength, and a thin thread of relief went through Charlotte. "How are you feeling?"

"Like I've been shot," he mumbled.

She ran her hand over his forehead, leaving a bloody smear, as Ren stood and moved away. "You're going to be just fine. I'll get us both out of this, okay?"

"Just stay quiet and do exactly what they tell you, Charlotte. They'll kill you if you don't," Vince said in a low voice.

She squeezed his hand. "I'm not afraid. And I don't want you to be afraid either."

She cried out with pain when a hand twisted into her long, blonde hair, and she was yanked to her feet. Steve pulled back her head, and she wrinkled her nose as his stale, tobacco-infused breath washed over her.

"What the fuck are you saying to that pig?"

"I was just telling him he would be fine," she gritted out as he pulled her hair tighter.

"You're a pretty little thing, ain't ya?" Steve suddenly crooned. He rubbed his finger across her cheek.

For the first time in three months, an emotion broke through the blank numbness that had enveloped her like a thick blanket. She was afraid for Vince. She didn't want Mel to lose him like she had lost Rick.

The thought of her imminent death brought on that same feeling of relief from before, and she had a moment to understand just how broken she really was before Ren was standing in front of them.

"Let her go."

"Since when did you care about some skinny little bitch?" Steve said

"Let her go," Ren repeated as the sirens wailed closer.

"You gonna make me?" Steve said.

"If I have to," Ren said.

After a long, tense minute, Steve snorted and thrust her towards Ren so roughly she would have fallen if he hadn't caught her. He held her against his large body, one hard arm wrapped around her waist and his big hand resting on her hip, as the sirens stopped abruptly.

"They're here." He pulled Charlotte towards the window and carefully peered behind the shade. He swore violently and stared at Steve as Jasper joined them in the salon.

"The back door is locked. But there are cops in the alley," he said.

"There are three cars out front. We've lost our chance." Ren glared at Steve.

"We've got a dying cop and four other hostages. They'll do whatever we ask them to do," Steve said.

"Jesus, Steve! Are you even listening to yourself?" Ren snarled. "We are in serious trouble here. You need to -"

Steve pointed his gun at him, and Charlotte felt Ren stiffen before he eased her behind him. "Don't be an asshole, Steve."

"No, don't *you* be an asshole, Ren." Steve wiped his nose and glared at him. "Who the fuck is in charge here? Huh? Is it you? Because I certainly don't remember giving up my rightful place as club president."

Ren, one hand still holding Charlotte, said, "You're in charge, Steve. I'm just trying to be helpful."

"Keep your fucking mouth shut then!" Steve said.

"Steve, man, we gotta do something," Jasper whined.

"Shut up!" Steve shouted. The shrill ring of the telephone made him jump, and he turned towards it.

"That'll be the police," Ren said. "You need to answer it, Steve."

Steve took a deep breath and glanced around the salon before reaching for the phone. "Everyone just stay the fuck quiet."

# CHAPTER 2

C harlotte tucked another cape around Vince's body and readjusted her sweater under his head. She squeezed his shoulder. "How are you doing, Vince?"

"Fine." His face was pale, but his voice was strong enough, and she took a deep breath before smiling at him.

"We'll get you to the hospital soon. Mel will be there waiting for you."

"Yeah." He cleared his throat. "I love her so much, Charlotte."

"I know you do, honey. She loves you too."

He squinted up at her. "How are you doing?"

"I'm fine. Don't worry about me," she said. She glanced behind her at Steve, sniffing a line of fine white powder from the top of the smooth reception desk. "If he keeps snorting that shit up his nose, I'll be able just to walk up and take the guns from him."

Vince frowned. "Don't do anything stupid, Charlotte. These guys are dangerous."

She glanced at Jasper, sitting on the floor beside Rita's station, and then at Ren, leaning against the far wall. His arms were folded over his chest, and he stared silently at them.

"Do you know the tall one?" she said.

Vince shook his head. "No."

"Are you sure?"

"Yes." He turned his head and gave Ren his own quick look. "He seems the most stable of the three of them, though."

"Yeah," she said. "Of course, that's not saying much, is it? Are they part of the motorcycle gang you mentioned earlier?"

Vince nodded and then coughed weakly before wincing. Charlotte frowned. Vince was doing remarkably well after being shot in the side, but he needed a hospital. She started to stand, and Vince took a ragged breath.

"Where are you going?"

"I'll be right back." She stood and walked toward Ren. He didn't move, and although he looked relaxed, she sensed the tense energy in his lean body hovering just below the surface.

"He needs to go to the hospital," she said.

When he didn't reply, she said, "He is going to die. Do you understand that? Or have you snorted too much coke like your idiot friend?"

"Be quiet, lady."

"Your friend is going to get us all killed," she said. "It's been nearly five hours, and he has no idea what he's doing. You heard him talking to the hostage negotiator. He's useless."

When he continued to stay silent, she stepped a little closer. "You seem like a smart guy, and maybe your brain hasn't been completely addled by the drugs yet. Why are you letting him run things? Are you that weak? That afraid of him?"

He surprised her by suddenly grinning, revealing even white teeth. "Maybe you should be a hostage negotiator. It's a good technique – trying to use our egos to turn us against each other."

She flushed. "I'm just asking you a simple question. Maybe you should -"

His eyes widened a fraction of a second before Steve grabbed her hair and shoved her to her knees. He put the barrel of his gun in the middle of her forehead.

"Did I give you permission to speak to my boy?" He cocked his gun as Darlene made a small moan of dismay, and Rita and Helen sobbed quietly.

The cold muzzle of the gun digging into her forehead, Charlotte stared up at the dirty, blond man. His eyes were wild, and he sniffed continually as he pushed the gun against her forehead.

"Beg me for your life, you stupid little bitch," he said.

She realized with sudden clarity that he was about to kill her, and she was helpless to stop the small smile of relief from crossing her face. She closed her eyes and waited for the darkness.

"Stop it, Steve." Ren's deep voice washed over her, and she felt the muzzle of the gun waver from her skin as Steve looked at him.

"Christ, this bitch wants to die. You can see it in her eyes." Steve made a high-pitched yodelling laugh.

"Get away from her." Ren's voice was deceptively soft as he pushed his body away from the wall.

"Why are you so fond of this skinny little whore?" Steve grabbed Charlotte's arm and yanked her to her feet. He dragged her to the other women and pushed her down beside them.

Rita buried her face in her shoulder, and Charlotte

wrapped her arms around the woman as Steve stared down at them.

He looked at Jasper and then at Ren, a slow grin creeping onto his face. "Let's play a game."

Jasper, leaning over the desk and taking a snort of white powder, straightened and scrubbed his hand across his nose. "What kind of game?"

Charlotte could see Ren tensing behind Steve as the smaller man grinned at her. "The kind that will have this cold little bitch all fired up."

"Don't be ridiculous, Steve," Ren growled. "This is neither the time nor the place."

"It never is. Is it, Ren?" Steve snapped. "How many women have I paraded in front of you, and you ain't fucked one of them."

"I don't need you choosing a woman for me."

Steve stepped closer to Charlotte, sliding the muzzle of his gun through her blonde hair. "Maybe you like boys."

When Ren refused to be goaded by him, Steve squatted down and smiled at Charlotte. "What's your name, bitch?"

"Charlotte."

"Pretty name for a pretty girl." He ran his dirty finger across her mouth. "Do you know that I took this asshole in? Gave him shelter and food, allowed him into my club, and shared freely with him everything that I worked so hard to acquire."

He smiled at her. "I've offered him woman after woman – all prettier than you – and he's turned each of them down. He insults my generosity by acting like he's too good to fuck one of my women. What do you think of a man who refuses to accept such a generous gift from the man who has given him so much?"

When she remained quiet, he yanked on her hair. "Answer me!"

"I think he's a fool."

He laughed. "Oh, I do like you." He glanced behind him at Ren. "And I think he likes you too."

He stood and turned to Ren. "Tell you what, old friend. I'm going to give you one last chance to prove your loyalty to me."

He waved his gun at Charlotte. "Stand up, bitch."

She untangled herself from Rita's grip and stood, walking forward when Steve motioned the gun at her.

"You're going to fuck her."

Ren stiffened. "No, I'm not."

Steve shrugged. "Fine, then I'll kill her."

He raised the gun and pointed it at Charlotte.

"Don't be a goddamn idiot, Steve. You're so fucking high right now you don't know what the hell you're doing," Ren said. "What do you think all those cops out there will do if they hear a gunshot? You start killing hostages, and we're finished."

Steve laughed. "I've still got four more hostages, Ren. They hear a gunshot, and all they'll do is phone again and try and talk me into giving myself up."

"What do you think, Charlotte?" Steve smiled at her. "He ain't a bad lookin' man. One quick fuck - or death. Make your choice."

She stared silently at him, and Steve laughed again. "This bitch is crazy! Jasper, you ever seen a bitch want to die so bad in your life?"

Jasper shook his head no as Steve turned back to Ren. "What'll it be? You going to have this woman's death on your conscience?"

Ren shrugged. "You said it yourself. The woman wants to die."

"Now you're both just bein' difficult," Steve said with a sullen pout.

"I'm not playing your game, Steve," Ren said.

"Oh, you'll play. And so will she." Steve pointed the gun at Vince. "The rules are changing. You fuck her – hell, fuck any of these bitches - to prove your loyalty to me, or I'll kill the cop."

Charlotte inhaled sharply, and Steve grinned at her. "That got you, didn't it?"

He looked at Ren. "Ready to play now, Ren?"

Ren shrugged again. "What the hell do I care about the life of some cop? Go ahead and kill him."

"Suit yourself." Steve started to stride towards Vince.

"Wait! I'll play the game." Charlotte said.

She could hear the fear in her voice as Steve stopped a few feet from Vince. "Christ, she's practically begging you for it now, Ren."

Steve yodelled laughter again. He waved the gun at Charlotte, and she walked over and stood next to Ren.

Vince struggled to sit up before falling back to the floor and panting. "Charlotte, don't do this. I'd rather die."

"Be quiet, Vince," Charlotte said.

"Play the game, Ren," Steve said. "Prove your loyalty, and I'll let the cop and your new little fuck buddy live. Go on now."

Ren stared down at her before taking her hand and leading her to the back of the salon.

"Where the hell do you think you're going?" Steve said.

Ren turned and stared at Steve steadily. "I'm not fucking her in front of you."

Steve eyed him shrewdly. "Fine. But if you even think of letting the cops in through the back or letting that bitch go, know that I'll kill the cop and at least one of these other bitches before they take me down. You get what I'm sayin'?"

"I get it," Ren said. He pulled Charlotte past the curtain that separated the back room from the salon.

* * *

Ren dropped her hand as soon as they were alone in the dim back room. Charlotte backed away from him until she was standing against the dryer. She ran her hands over her skirt and stared quietly at him as he paced back and forth.

"Fuck!" He slammed his hand against the metal shelving that held their extra products, and she winced when bottles of shampoo and conditioner clattered to the floor.

He stared at the small, blonde woman in the pink blouse and grey skirt. Her dark brown eyes regarded him steadily, and she looked remarkably unafraid. He slammed his fist into his thigh and stared at the tile floor. He had no idea what to do. He had never taken a woman against her will in his life and would never be able to. Just the thought of forcing her to do something she didn't want to made his skin crawl.

He slammed his fist into his thigh again. He knew without a doubt that Steve would kill the cop and the woman standing in front of him. Killing the cop was bad enough, but the thought of watching Steve shoot Charlotte in the head sent a surprisingly large flood of dismay through him.

He glanced at Charlotte again. Despite his inner turmoil, he was ridiculously attracted to her. Had been since the moment they had entered the salon. He cursed himself for allowing that attraction to be so readily noticeable to Steve. If he had kept his emotions in check, they wouldn't be in this goddamn mess right now.

"What are you waiting for?" she said.

"I can't do this," he said. "I'm sorry, but there's no way in hell I can have sex with you."

She crossed her arms over her chest. "You have to."

"I can't," he repeated.

17

"If you don't, Vince will die. You heard your idiot friend – he'll kill him," she said.

"I have never forced myself on a woman, and I'm not going to start now," he gritted out.

"It's not forced. I'm willing."

"Lying is not going to help the situation."

She boosted herself up on the top of the dryer until she was sitting on the edge of it, her slender legs dangling over the side. "I'm not lying. I want you to do this."

He stalked over to her. "That's bullshit, and you know it."

"I won't let him die! Do you get that?" She unexpectedly punched him hard in the chest, and he winced.

"Yeah, I get that. But you need to understand that I can't take a woman by force. Even if I could get my brain to forget how goddamn horrible the idea is, a certain part of my anatomy will not forget it. Do you get that?"

"Then make it nice."

He blinked at her in confusion as she glared at him. "You're not entirely unattractive. I won't come, but we can at least make it so it won't hurt. At this point, that's the best we can hope for."

He glanced at the ring on her left hand. "You're married."

She swallowed hard. "I'm a widow."

"When did he die?"

"That's none of your business," she said.

"I'm sorry for your loss."

"Yeah, thanks." Her soft voice was thick with sarcasm. "C'mon, we need to get this over with."

She ignored his wince. "You and I both know your coked-out friend is going to come back here at any minute and if we're not having sex, he'll kill Vince."

When he continued to hesitate, she rolled her eyes and yanked him up against the dryer. She wrapped her legs around his waist and then pushed his chin up roughly before burying her face in his neck.

He shuddered with pleasure at the first touch of her soft lips against his throat. She placed gentle kisses against his throat before licking him like a cat with her small, pink tongue. He released his breath in an explosive rush as she shifted until her small body pressed more firmly against him.

His cock hardened almost immediately. It had been well over a year since he'd been with a woman, and he was intoxicated by the feel of Charlotte's soft body and warm mouth. Her sweet scent surrounded him, and he breathed deeply as she kissed his neck. She let her lips brush against his thick beard before she nibbled on his earlobe.

"Jesus," he muttered. He was only vaguely aware of her hands unbuttoning his vest until she had shoved it off of him and was yanking at the hem of his t-shirt. He lifted his arms so she could pull it free.

Her eyes widened at the multiple tattoos that covered his chest, torso and arms, but her hands were perfectly steady when she reached out and ran her fingers through the hair on his chest. He jerked his pelvis against her. His erection was obvious, and she stared at him with her dark eyes before sliding her hand inside his jeans and underwear. She gripped him firmly, and he moaned.

"Good," she breathed. She pulled her hand free and quickly unbuttoned her blouse. He stared hungrily at her small breasts in the lacy white bra.

"Touch them," she demanded.

He hesitated at the look in her eyes. Instead of being warm and hazy with desire, there was a terrible blankness in them that had his cock softening instantly.

"C'mon," she said, "they're very sensitive. Touching them will make me wet enough for you to enter me."

She grabbed his hands and placed them on her breasts. He pulled his hands away, and she frowned. "What?"

"Just give me a minute," he muttered.

"We don't have a minute." She scowled and tried to draw his hands back to her breasts. He refused and instead put his hands around her slender waist and tangled them in her long hair. He gently tugged until she looked up at the ceiling.

It didn't matter how many times she reassured him. There was no way he could have sex with her unless she wanted him as much as he wanted her. Just making her wet wasn't enough. The only way he'd even maintain an erection was if she was as hot for him as he was for her. He dipped his head toward her throat, saying a silent prayer that this would work.

She twitched against him when he nuzzled her neck, her fingers tightening a little in the hair on his chest. He kissed his way up her throat before trailing a path along her jaw. When he tried to kiss her full mouth, she darted her head back, hissing a little when it made her hair pull in his hands.

"No kissing on the mouth," she said.

He hesitated and then nodded his agreement before dipping his head and kissing his way down the other side of her throat. God, this was insanity and, without a doubt, a huge mistake. So why was he so eager to fuck her?

# CHAPTER 3

Charlotte stared at the ceiling as Ren trailed his firm lips across the top of her chest to her collarbone. He licked it lightly, and she was shocked to feel a thin thread of desire course through her. His beard tickled, and she had to stifle the moan in her throat when he moved one big hand to her flat stomach and rubbed gently.

Although Rick had died only three months ago, it had been nearly two years since they were intimate. The cancer and subsequent chemotherapy treatments and radiation had consumed their lives. Their previously frequent and active sex life had gradually dwindled to nothing. At the time, she hadn't cared. She had just wanted Rick alive and healthy.

Now, as the numbness from the last three months was slowly replaced with an aching need to touch and be touched, she tentatively placed her hands on Ren's shoulders. Her stomach was churning with a combination of shame and desire, and she cursed Ren violently in her head for making her want him. She wished bitterly for the numbness to be back. At least then, she wouldn't feel like she was cheating on her dead husband with a drug-addicted criminal.

*You're only doing this to save Vince's life. Rick would understand.*

But as Ren's hand drew maddeningly slow circles on her stomach, and she dug her hands into his broad shoulders to stop herself from forcing his hands onto her suddenly-aching breasts, she knew that was a lie. What she was doing might have started as a desperate attempt to save a man's life, but she would be a fool to try and convince herself it was the only reason now.

Ren's large hand suddenly covered her breast, his thumb rubbing almost lazily across her nipple, and she was helpless to stop the small moan from escaping her throat. He undid the front clasp of her bra, peeling it back to reveal her small, firm breasts.

With a trembling hand, he reached out and cupped her bare breast. Her nipple hardened immediately, and he made a soft groan of appreciation before plucking lightly at it with his fingers. Her back arched, and she pressed her pelvis eagerly against his, her legs tightening around his waist as he cupped both of her breasts and rubbed her sensitive nipples.

"Charlotte, look at me," Ren said.

Her eyes fluttered open, and she could almost see the anxiety in his gaze disappear. She knew her desire for him was written on her face. His cock was a hot hard length against her, and he groaned when she rubbed herself against it.

His mouth bent to hers, but before she could remind him about the no kissing rule, he changed course and kissed her cheek instead before licking the curve of her ear. He sucked hard on her earlobe, running his hands up and down her back under her blouse as she pressed herself against him. Her naked breasts, their nipples hard little points, brushed against his chest, and his hands tightened almost painfully into her soft skin.

"Ren," she moaned.

He bent and took one hard nipple into his mouth. She made another loud moan and clutched at his head as he first nipped and then sucked hard on her nipple. He moved to her other one as she rocked her hips frantically against him.

Her motions had pushed her skirt up to the middle of her thighs, and as he continued to suck on her nipple, he reached between their bodies and stroked her soft thigh. She shifted against the dryer, and he slipped his hand under her crumpled skirt, skated his fingers past the silky material of her panties and cupped her warm pussy.

She gasped, her eyes popping open as her legs tightened helplessly around his hips. She stared up at him, and he moved his fingers slowly across her embarrassingly wet pussy lips. She reached between them and grabbed his wrist.

"Should I stop?" he said hoarsely.

She hesitated and shook her head no, her hand loosening and falling away. He moved his fingers to her clit. It was hard and swollen, and she moaned loudly when he rubbed it.

He lifted her off the dryer, and she reached under her skirt and shoved her underwear down her thighs. He pulled them down her legs, and she impatiently kicked them off one foot, letting them dangle from her other ankle as he unbuttoned and unzipped his jeans and pulled his cock free.

Charlotte looked down, feeling the hot blush rising on her face at the sight of his large cock jutting out of his jeans. The numbness that had swallowed her for so long was completely gone now. It had been replaced by a fiery lust for the man standing between her legs.

She'd forgotten about being a hostage, about Vince bleeding on the floor, about Steve and his games. As she wrapped her legs around Ren's waist again and urged him toward her, she could think of nothing but finding relief from the aching throb in her pelvis. It had been too long since she had felt anything but sorrow and pain and numbness, and the desire flowing through her body was as addictive to her as Steve's cocaine was to him.

"Please," she panted.

Ren pulled her forward and lifted her legs a bit higher around his waist before reaching between them and guiding his cock into her wet and slick entrance. His large size stretched her tightness, and she couldn't hold in her hiss of pain as she squeezed her legs around his waist. He stopped immediately, his hand brushing her hair back from her face.

"I'm sorry," he said.

"It's fine. Just give me a minute to adjust to the size," she said.

He reached between them and ran his fingers over her clit. She shivered in his arms as she tipped her head back so that he could place warm, wet kisses on the column of her throat. She relaxed her legs, and he pushed forward. They made mutual low groans when his cock slid further into her. He continued to rub her clit, bringing her closer and closer to climaxing as he gently pressed forward until his entire cock was seated inside her.

He drew in a deep, ragged breath as he put both hands on her hips and held her tight. She draped her arms over his shoulders, locking her hands behind his neck, and stared at him as he slid in and out.

"Harder," she said.

"I don't want to hurt you," he said in a low voice.

"You won't." She squeezed her pussy around his thick cock, a little shiver going down her back when he groaned loudly.

Still, he withdrew and oh so slowly plunged into her. She stared up at him, and as he pulled back and surged into her again, he dipped his head to kiss her.

He stopped at the last moment, his mouth hovering over hers and her breath warm on his lips. With a sigh of frustration, he moved his head back. Feeling an odd sense of madness, she clamped her hands around his neck. He groaned when she tilted her mouth towards his and licked his lips with her soft tongue.

"Charlotte, please," he moaned.

She wanted to kiss him. It was stupid to pretend she didn't. She pressed her mouth against his, her tongue darting past his open lips. He groaned again and cupped the back of her head, holding her firmly as he kissed her. He shoved his tongue into her mouth, stroking hers roughly as he kissed and licked and nipped at her full lips.

He thrust into her, his movements turning harder and faster. The dryer she was sitting on was rocking back and forth, making a loud hollow thump every time it banged against the wall. Charlotte kissed Ren hard. He tasted so good. A drug-dealing biker shouldn't taste this good. His tongue swept through her mouth again, and she opened it wide so that he could taste every inch of it.

He was moving faster now, his hips thrusting furiously against hers. She was so close, and she whimpered her need as he slipped his hand between their bodies. His rough fingers rubbed her clit, and she arched her back, crying out into his mouth as her orgasm raced through her. Her pussy clamped down on his hard cock, and with his own short cry, he pulled her flush against him, pumped rapidly in and out twice more and climaxed.

She collapsed against him, feeling his harsh breath against her hair as he stroked her back. After a moment, he leaned back a little and stared down at her. He surprised her by cupping her face and kissing her sweetly. She kissed him back, her body still shuddering with the force of her climax.

"Aww, ain't that the sweetest thing I ever saw."

Ren froze against her and turned his head. He kept her close to his body, hiding her nakedness behind his broad back.

"I only caught the last few minutes, but it looked like the little bitch enjoyed herself," Steve said. "You got a way with the bitches don't ya, Ren?"

"Get out," Ren said.

"Hold on now. Maybe I should take a turn. See if I can make her feel as good as you did," Steve said.

"I didn't take you for a man who enjoyed sloppy seconds," Ren said.

"Fuck you, Ren." Steve wiped at his nose again. "You'd be wise to remember I'm the one with the guns."

Faintly, they could hear the phone ring, and Ren stared at Steve. "That'll be for you."

"Yeah. You got three minutes to get your asses back out there." Steve left the back room.

Ren stepped away from Charlotte as she quickly did up her bra and then buttoned her blouse. He zipped his jeans and pulled his shirt and vest back on before hooking her panties around her other foot and pulling them up to her thighs. Before she could hop down from the dryer, he lifted her and set her gently on her feet. She pulled her panties up under her skirt and started toward the door.

He took her arm. "Wait."

She watched as he bent and lifted the leg of his jeans. He had a leather holster around his calf, a gun tucked firmly in it, and she blinked in surprise as he quickly undid it and knelt at her feet. He slipped it under her skirt and gently pushed her thighs apart.

"What are you doing?" she whispered.

He wrapped the holster around one smooth thigh and buckled it. It barely fit, and she winced as the stiff leather bit into her soft skin. He stood up and stepped back, staring critically at her. Her skirt's soft, full folds hid the bulk of the gun nicely.

"Ren? What are you doing?"

He surprised her by pulling her into his arms and cupping her face. He bent his head, and she opened her mouth in anticipation of his kiss. Instead of kissing her, he breathed into her ear, "If he takes you back here, if he tries anything, do not hesitate to shoot him. Do you understand me?"

"I've never fired a gun in my life," she said.

"The safety is off. Just put your finger on the trigger, aim for his chest and squeeze."

"You want me to shoot your friend?"

"He's not my friend," he growled. "When we go back out there, stay quiet and don't antagonize him. Ignore everything he says, okay?"

She nodded. The weight of the gun around her thigh felt strange, and she reached down and touched it lightly through the material of her skirt.

He shook his head. "No, don't do that. Steve's a coke addict, but he's also a goddamn psychopath and too sharp for his own good. Just keep your hands away from it."

"Who are you?" she said.

"I'm no one. Just an asshole who got himself involved with the wrong crowd." He kissed her roughly, his tongue slipping between her lips and tangling with hers before he stepped back.

"C'mon." He took her hand and led her out of the back room.

\* \* \*

"I DON'T CARE WHAT THE FUCK YOU SAY. IF YOU DON'T WANT A dead cop, you'll do exactly what I want!" When Ren led

Charlotte back into the salon, Steve was yelling into the phone. Ren held her hand tightly until Charlotte, blushing a little at the look Helen gave her, yanked her hand free and walked over to Vince.

She sat down beside him and stroked his forehead gently.

"I'm so sorry, Charlotte," Vince wheezed.

"It's fine, Vince."

"Did he hurt you?"

Before she could answer, his eyes rolled up, and his head slumped.

"Vince?" Panic bloomed in her belly when his eyes didn't open. She leaned over him. "Vincent! Open your eyes!"

Ren was suddenly kneeling beside her, placing his fingers on Vince's neck. "He's just unconscious."

She peeled back the cape covering him and made a small moan of dismay at the amount of blood that had soaked through the towels. "He's going to die if we don't get him to the hospital."

"I know," Ren said, his voice grim. "Go and sit with the others."

She stood and joined the other women as Ren crossed the salon and spoke quietly to Jasper.

Charlotte watched them until the burn of Helen's gaze became too much to ignore. She turned to Helen, who stared at her with undisguised disgust. "What?"

"Nothing," Helen said.

"You obviously have something to say, so say it," she said.

"We heard you back there with that... that criminal, Charlotte. What would Rick have said if -"

"Shut up, Helen!" Darlene said. "Charlotte didn't have a choice. They would have killed Vince and her if she hadn't gone back there with him. She was pretending."

"Yeah, well, she's one hell of an actress then," Helen said

28

"You're a stupid old cow!" Darlene said in a low voice. Charlotte laid a hand on Darlene's arm as Helen flushed.

"I'm not the one who just had sex with a criminal three months after my husband died," Helen said.

"She didn't have a choice. He was going to kill her," Darlene said.

"Yeah, well, I would rather die than let that animal touch me." Helen glared at her.

"Both of you shut up!" Rita whispered as Steve slammed down the phone.

He scowled at Jasper and Ren. "What the hell are you sons of bitches so chummy about?"

Ren glanced up. "Nothing, Steve. We're just trying to figure out a way to get out of this mess alive."

Steve snorted. "I got it all under control. They're going to be bringing us a helicopter."

Ren rolled his eyes. "Jesus Christ, Steve, you really are an idiot."

"I've had just about enough of your smart mouth, Ren," Steve said.

"They're not going to give you a helicopter," Ren said. "If you don't start handing over hostages, they won't give you anything. Send the cop out as a gesture of goodwill. If you don't, they're going to come busting in here and kill us. I promise you that."

"We got hostages! They ain't gonna do nothin' to us!" There was uncertainty in Steve's voice.

"It's been nearly five hours. You're making unreasonable demands and refusing to give them anything in return. Trust me, with every minute that passes, the hostages become more and more expendable to the cops."

"How the hell do you know all this shit?" Steve said.

"I watch a lot of crime shows," Ren said impatiently. "Pick up the phone, Steve. Tell them you're sending out the cop."

Steve hesitated, glancing first at Vince and then at the women sitting against the wall.

"No," he said. "That cop is the only leverage we have. They ain't gonna care about a bunch of bitches. If we give up the cop, we're all dead."

"We're already dead," Ren said. "You're just too stupid to realize it."

"You know what, Ren? I don't think we need you in the club anymore."

Steve raised his gun and pointed it at him. Before he could fire, the salon's front window exploded with a loud bang. Charlotte scrambled to her feet and ran for Vince as the other women screamed and threw themselves to the floor.

Two long grey canisters shot through the broken window and past the shredded blind, landing with a soft clatter in the middle of the room. There were two more bangs, these so loud that Charlotte's ears began to ring, accompanied by bright flashes that momentarily blinded her. The room filled with smoke. Faintly, she could hear Steve cursing and coughing and the other women shrieking.

Coughing on the acrid smoke, her eyes watering so badly she could barely see, Charlotte tripped over the chair at Rita's station and went sprawling. She staggered to her feet, and suddenly, Ren stood before her. He grabbed her arm as a gunshot rang out, and the mirror shattered behind them.

"Shit!" Ren yelled. He tried to push her to the ground. "Charlotte - get down!"

"No! I need to get to Vince!" She yanked out of her grip and ran for Vince.

"Dammit, Charlotte, wait!" Ren's fingers brushed against the sleeve of Charlotte's shirt but couldn't catch hold. Before he could chase after her, there was another gunshot, and he watched her tiny body shake violently as she stumbled back. There was pain in his chest, and he looked down to see blood oozing through his white t-shirt as she turned around to face him.

"Ren?" she whispered.

His eyes widened as a matching patch of blood appeared on the front of her pink blouse. He forgot about his wound and rushed forward as she started to collapse. He caught her, panic blooming in his belly at the amount of blood pouring out of her shoulder.

"You're dead, asshole." Steve appeared behind Charlotte, pointing his gun at Ren's head. He pulled the trigger, cursing when there was only a dry click. Ren shoved his hand under Charlotte's skirt and pulled his gun free from the holster around her thigh as Steve reached for Vince's gun tucked into his belt.

"Fuck you, Steve." Ren squinted through the smoke and fired his weapon as men wearing helmets and face shields burst through the broken window of the salon. Steve clapped his hand to his side, looking in disbelief at the blood covering his hand before falling to the floor.

His legs suddenly too weak to hold him, Ren sank to the floor, holding Charlotte tightly and dropping the gun on the floor next to them. He leaned over her, fighting off the sudden fog clouding his brain. "Charlotte? Stay awake, honey."

"Hurts," she moaned.

"I know, baby." His chest throbbed and burned, and it was suddenly tough to breathe. "Stay awake, okay? Don't -"

He cried out as she was ripped away from him and he was shoved to the ground.

"Down on the floor! Down on the floor!" Three men held guns to his head, and he groaned with pain as they flipped him onto his stomach and yanked his hands behind his back, cuffing them tightly. As darkness crept over his vision, he turned his head, searching for Charlotte. The last thing he saw before the darkness claimed him was Charlotte lying in a growing pool of her own blood, her dark eyes staring gravely at him.

# CHAPTER 4

Charlotte groaned and forced her heavy eyelids open. She stared blearily at the white ceiling as a soft beeping filled her ears, groaning again when she realized where she was. She had spent enough time in them over the last two years to recognize a hospital room when she saw one.

She turned her head, licking her dry lips, and stared at the IV pole beside the bed. She was searching for the call button when a shadow fell over her. She looked upwards, a small smile crossing her face when she saw Melody's soft and pretty features.

She tried to say Mel's name, but nothing would come out.

"Here, sweetie. It's only a couple of ice chips, but it will help." Melody popped the ice chips into her mouth, and Charlotte felt a surge of love for the small, dark-haired woman as the ice chips slowly melted and trickled down her dry and dusty throat.

"Vince?" she whispered.

"He's fine," Mel said. "He's on a different floor, but he's recovering nicely. He's already driving the nurses crazy."

ELIZABETH KELLY

Charlotte smiled a little. Already, she was growing tired, and her left shoulder burned and throbbed, but she fought against the weariness. A memory of the grey-eyed Ren holding her and telling her to stay awake drifted across her mind, and she forced her drooping eyelids open again.

"What happened to Ren?" she rasped.

Mel hesitated. "Sweetie, you need to rest."

She was too weary to argue. Mel placed a cool hand on her forehead. "You lost a lot of blood when you were shot. Go to sleep, sweetie."

Charlotte closed her eyes and drifted.

* * *

"Hey. Feeling better?" Vince sat in the chair next to her hospital bed when she opened her eyes.

She squinted at him for a moment before a nurse hovered over her. "Hello, Charlotte. I'm Lara. How do you feel? Do you think you'd like to sit up a bit? Maybe drink some water?"

Before Charlotte could reply, there was a soft buzzing noise, and she felt the upper half of the bed slowly rise.

"You'll feel a bit light-headed. That's completely normal. You've been lying flat on your back for the last two days. Now, don't try to move your left arm. We've got it bandaged against your body for a reason."

Lara brought a Styrofoam cup with a straw sticking out of it to her mouth. "Take small sips, please."

She sipped obediently. The cool water tasted wonderful, but Lara pulled the cup away before she could drink all of it. "That's enough for now."

She glanced at Vince. "You can give her the other half in about ten minutes, okay?"

34

He nodded, and Lara patted Charlotte's leg before leaving the room.

Vince and Charlotte stared silently at each other for a few moments before Charlotte gave him a small smile.

"Hi."

"Hi, sweetie." Vince, wincing a little, scooted his chair closer to the bed to hold her hand.

"How are you feeling?" Charlotte said.

"Good. The doctor dug the bullet out. I lost my spleen, and I have to take a month's medical leave, but it could have been worse."

"I guess. What happened?" She glanced at her heavily bandaged arm trapped in a sling against her chest.

"You were shot in the shoulder by that dickhead Steve." Vince squeezed her hand. "By the time they got you into surgery, you had already lost a lot of blood. They thought you were going to -"

He paused and cleared his throat. "They gave you a shit-load of blood transfusions, took you into surgery to repair the damage from the bullet, and sewed you back up. And here you are – as good as new."

"Here I am," she repeated. "Are the others okay?"

He nodded. "Yeah. Darlene came by yesterday to see you – those flowers are from her. I guess Rita and Helen are still pretty shaken up, but they're not hurt."

"Good." She sighed and closed her eyes for a minute. "What about…"

"Steve and Jasper are alive. Steve was shot, but it didn't do much damage. They're in prison, waiting for their trial."

"We'll have to testify, won't we?" Charlotte said.

He nodded and rubbed his jaw wearily. "Yeah, sweetie, we will. But that won't be for a while."

"What about Ren?"

"When Steve shot you, the bullet went right through you

and lodged in Ren's lung. They took him into surgery, but he - he died on the table," Vince said.

Charlotte looked down at her lap. She could feel tears threatening, and she blinked them back rapidly, afraid of what Vince would think of her if he saw her crying over one of the men who had nearly gotten them killed. Hell, she didn't understand it herself. Ren was a drug addict and a criminal and had held them hostage for almost six hours.

She should be grateful he had died, but she couldn't stop thinking about how gentle he had been with her. He could have hurt her, could have forced her to have sex with him without caring what it did to her, but instead, he'd been kind and almost sweet in the back room of the salon.

"Charlotte? Sweetie, are you okay?" Vince asked.

"I'm fine." She lifted her head and forced herself to smile at him.

"He was a bad guy, Charlotte."

"Was he?" she said.

"He took you into the back room and," he swallowed heavily, "he raped you."

"It wasn't rape, Vince." Feeling the blush rising in her cheeks, she made herself go on. "I don't know what happened, call it temporary insanity, or hell, maybe it had just been so long since I'd felt anything but numbness that I didn't care who or what he was, but he didn't rape me. I wanted the sex just as much as he did."

"He didn't force you?" Vince's face had paled.

"No. He couldn't. In fact, the only way I could get him even to touch me was by reminding him that you were going to die if he didn't."

Vince flinched. "I'm so sorry, Charlotte. This was my fault."

She sighed impatiently. "No, that isn't what I meant. I was just trying to explain to you that what happened with Ren wasn't rape. He was gentle and – and kind even. He might have been a drug addict and maybe a horrible human being, but he wasn't a rapist."

She had no idea why she was so desperate to defend Ren's behaviour with her. He was dead, after all. And even if he had been alive, he probably wouldn't have worried that much about his reputation.

"He gave me a gun."

"What?" Vince stared at her in shock.

"Steve came in after we… were finished in the back room. He threatened to take his turn with me, and Ren told him to back off. Steve went to answer the phone, and Ren had a gun in a holster around his calf. He buckled it to my thigh and told me that if Steve brought me back into this room, to shoot him. He told me to aim for his chest and squeeze the trigger."

"Jesus." Vince ran his hand over his face again and then stood abruptly. He winced and put a hand to his side.

"Vince? Are you okay?"

"I'm fine. Listen, I have to go. I have to make a phone call before it's too late."

She frowned. "What are you talking about?"

"Don't worry about it, okay? I'll be back later this afternoon. Get some rest."

# CHAPTER 5

T*en months later*

CHARLOTTE TOOK A DEEP BREATH AND STEPPED OUT OF THE car. Vince and Mel stood on the sidewalk waiting for her, and they quickly formed a shield around her as the throng of reporters crowded close.

The three of them walked rapidly up the courthouse steps and into the large building without speaking. Charlotte breathed a sigh of relief when the doors closed behind them, shutting out the reporters and their shouted questions.

"Are you ready, sweetie?" Vince asked.

"Yes." Her legs trembled, and sweat formed on her upper lip.

"Are you sure?" Mel said.

"Yes. I'm ready to have this over with. I'm the prosecutor's last witness. After today, I don't ever have to think about those assholes again," Charlotte said.

A hand touched her shoulder. "Hello, Charlotte."

She smiled at the crown prosecutor. "Hi, Michael."

"You look good."

She flushed a little under his gaze, and his cheeks reddened. "I mean, you look very uh – formal. It's good for a court appearance."

"Thanks."

He nodded briefly at Vince and Mel before putting his hand on the small of Charlotte's back and ushering her forward. "We've got a few minutes. I want to go over your testimony once more. Are you okay with that?"

She nodded, her body practically vibrating with nerves. He smiled down at her, his dark brown eyes warm and full of confidence. "You'll be fine. Remember to keep your answers short, and don't let him fluster you. Just like we've been practicing, okay?"

She took another deep breath as he led her to a quiet spot down the hall. "Okay."

"Good, that was perfect," Michael said a few minutes later. "I know you're nervous, but you sound confident, and that's important."

"I'm past nervous and moving into terrified," Charlotte said.

"That's normal, but you're going to do great. I'll question you first, and there won't be any surprises. It'll be all the questions we rehearsed together. Then, it'll be the defense attorney's turn. Just remember to stay calm and don't let him trip you up. The key is to keep your answers as short as possible. Don't do any elaborating, okay?"

"Yup. I've got this. I think."

He reached out and squeezed her hands. "I know you do."

"Thanks." There was an awkward moment before he released her hands.

"Listen, Charlotte, after this is over, I was wondering if you might like to get a drink with me?" Michael said.

She blinked at him in surprise. "Oh, um, yeah, I guess I could do that."

He smiled boyishly at her. "Great. That's really great."

* * *

"Ms. Montgomery, I'd like to talk about what happened in the back room of the salon." The defense attorney gave her a shark-like smile.

Charlotte tensed and then made herself take a deep breath. She had known he would bring it up. Michael had skipped over it but warned her that the defense attorney would not. Her gaze fell on Jasper and Steve sitting at the defense table. They were both dressed in suits, and Steve's long hair was tied back neatly. Jasper only stared sullenly at her, but Steve gave her a wide grin before making a kissing motion.

She looked away as the defense attorney approached her. "Ms. Montgomery?"

"Yes?"

"We've heard testimony from the other witnesses – your coworkers and police officer Vince Shallen - that my client insisted you play a game with one of the club members, Renfrew Flynn?"

"Yes," Charlotte said.

"Can you tell the court what that game was?"

She took another deep breath. "Your client told Ren that if he didn't have sex with me, he would kill Vince and me."

"I see. And what happened then?"

"Ren refused. Steve was about to kill Vince, and I shouted at him to stop, that I would play the game," Charlotte said.

"And then?" The defense attorney prompted.

She took a quick look at Michael, who nodded reassur-

41

ingly to her. "Ren took me to the back room of the salon, and we had sex."

"You mean he raped you."

"No. It wasn't rape."

"Not rape?" The defense attorney cocked his head at her. "You mean you willingly had sex with Mr. Flynn?"

"Yes."

"Ms. Montgomery, you must forgive me, but I'm confused. This man was part of a well-known club of drug dealers and murderers and had been holding you hostage for five hours, but you, a woman who's never even gotten a parking ticket, willingly had sex with him."

"Yes." Charlotte could feel the bright blush heating her skin, and she had an almost undeniable urge to try to explain her actions to the prosecutor and the rest of the people sitting in the large courtroom. She bit the inside of her cheek and suppressed the urge fiercely.

"Were you frightened, Ms. Montgomery?"

"Yes."

"But not frightened enough to keep you from having sex with one of the men holding you hostage?"

"I didn't have a choice. They were going to kill Vince."

"Tell me what happened after you went into the back room with Mr. Flynn."

"He told me he couldn't have sex with me, that he – he couldn't force himself on me. I told him that he didn't have a choice and that I wasn't going to let Vince die."

"What happened then?"

"I started kissing and touching him."

"And Mr. Flynn responded to your advances?"

"Yes."

"And then what?"

Suddenly impatient with his stupid questions, she rolled her eyes. "I already told you we had sex."

"You're a widow, are you not?" the defense attorney said.

She stiffened. "Yes."

"And how long had your husband been deceased before you had sex with Mr. Flynn?"

"Three months."

"So, let me see if I understand this. You had sex with the person holding you hostage and threatening your life three months after your husband died?"

"Objection, your honour!" Michael stood up. "What does her husband's death have to do with anything?"

"Sustained." The judge turned to the defense attorney. "Get to the point, Mr. Wall."

"Yes, your honour." He smiled at Charlotte. "Just a few more questions, Ms. Montgomery."

She nodded as he paced back and forth in front of her momentarily.

"Did you have an orgasm during sex with Mr. Flynn?" he said.

"Objection!" Michael was on his feet as Charlotte blushed again. "Your honour, Ms. Montgomery has already admitted to having consensual sex with one of the gang members. Why does the defense need her to go into such detail?"

"Your honour, three of Ms. Montgomery's coworkers testified that they were terrified for their lives. Ms. Montgomery herself testified earlier that she was frightened. They all indicated that my clients, Mr. Terrence and Mr. Logan, had threatened and tormented them into a state of gut-wrenching fear. Yet, Ms. Montgomery, despite her overwhelming fear, has admitted to having sex with one of the men who was holding them hostage. I'm trying to establish just how much of a threat my clients actually presented if one of the hostages willingly had sex with one of them."

"It's already been established that she did it because they

threatened to kill someone she cared for deeply," Michael said.

The judge held up his hand. "I'll allow the question." He turned to Charlotte. "Answer the question, Ms. Montgomery."

Charlotte swallowed. "Yes, I had an orgasm."

The defense attorney stared at her for a moment. "Tell me, Ms. Montgomery, did you know Mr. Flynn was an undercover detective?"

Charlotte's mouth dropped open, and she stared wordlessly at the man before her gaze fell on Vince and Mel, sitting in the front row just behind Michael.

"Ms. Montgomery?" The defense attorney said.

Charlotte stared at him. Her ears rang, and she thought for one horrifying moment that she might faint. She could feel Michael's worried gaze as the judge leaned closer.

"Ms. Montgomery, answer the question, please."

"No," she whispered. "I didn't know that."

"Huh. So, at no point during your rendezvous with him in the back room did Detective Flynn mention he was an undercover detective?"

"No," she said

"But you still had sex with him? Even though you believed that he was a club member."

"Yes."

"Interesting. Since you had no problem with having intercourse with one of the men holding you hostage and, in fact, were brought to orgasm by him, I wonder if perhaps my clients did not instill quite the amount of fear in you that you claim."

"Objection!" Michael barked.

"Sustained," the judge said. "The jury will disregard the last statement made by the defense."

As Michael sat back down, the defense attorney smiled at

Charlotte. "No further questions, your honour. Thank you, Ms. Montgomery. You've been very helpful."

The judge turned to Michael. "Would you like to cross-examine your witness, Mr. Winters?"

Michael nodded and jumped up. "Ms. Montgomery, were you frightened of Detective Flynn?"

"At first, but not once we were in the back room."

"Why not?"

"Because he was very, um, gentle and made it clear that he wouldn't hurt me."

"Thank you. And did Mr. Terrence make it clear that he wouldn't hurt you?" Michael asked.

"No. After we finished, Steve came into the back room. He commented about taking his turn, and Ren told him to leave. Steve reminded Ren that he needed to be careful and that he was the one with the guns. After he left, Ren took a gun he had hidden around his calf and strapped it to my thigh. He told me that if Steve took me into the back room and tried to hurt me, I was to shoot him."

"Did you find that strange?"

"Yes. I asked him who he was, and he said he was no one. He said he was just an asshole who got involved with the wrong crowd."

"Did you believe that Detective Flynn would harm you?"

"No."

"Did you believe that Mr. Terrence would harm you?"

"Yes. And I was right – he shot me."

"Thank you, Ms. Montgomery. I have no further questions, your honour." Michael sat down, and when the judge dismissed her, Charlotte stood and walked shakily to her seat. She hesitated and then sat down next to Vince in the front row.

"Charlotte -"

"Did you know, Vince? You did, didn't you?"

45

"Yes," he said. When she didn't reply, he placed a gentle hand on her arm, wincing when she jerked away from him. "Charlotte, I'm so sorry, I -"

"Be quiet, Vince." She stared down at her tightly clasped hands. "I can't talk to you right now."

"Charlotte -"

"Leave her alone, honey," Mel said gently.

Charlotte closed her eyes. Her heart was beating so fast and loud that she could barely hear the judge telling Michael to call his next witness. She frowned. She was the last witness. Wasn't she?

Michael cleared his throat. "The prosecution calls Detective Renfrew Flynn."

There was a collective gasp throughout the courtroom. Charlotte, her hands clammy and her stomach suddenly in her feet, turned to look behind her, the tendons in her neck creaking like old boards.

The door to the courtroom opened, and Ren walked through. Charlotte stared silently at him as he walked down the aisle separating the rows of seating. He wore a dark grey suit with a burgundy tie. His hair had been cut short, and the thick beard was gone. A thin scar ran across his chin and another just under the left side of his jaw.

He walked past without looking at her, and she turned back in her seat. The buzzing was back in her head, and the courtroom suddenly seemed too warm. She tried to gulp in air like a fish gulping water, but her lungs had stopped working. This time, she knew for sure she was going to faint.

Mel was suddenly sitting next to her. She put a cool hand on the back of Charlotte's neck and, in a sharp voice, said, "Put your head between your knees, sweetie."

She pushed Charlotte down and bent next to her. "Take deep breaths. C'mon, sweetie, in through the nose, out through the mouth. Nice and slow."

As Ren was sworn in, Charlotte listened to Mel's soft voice and concentrated on drawing air in and out of her beleaguered lungs.

* * *

CHARLOTTE STARED NUMBLY AT REN. MICHAEL HAD questioned him about his involvement with Steve's motorcycle club, and she was surprised to learn that he was deep undercover for over a year. Michael kept his questioning brief, asking questions that revealed the club's drug activity for the last year and the events leading to Vince being shot.

Despite her shock at Ren being an undercover cop and alive, Charlotte was still impressed by Michael's ability in the courtroom. With only a few simple questions, he had established just how dangerous and out of control Steve had been in the salon.

For the last fifteen minutes, she had watched the defense grill Ren. The attorney had barely mentioned the salon. Instead, he'd been questioning him on incidents that happened throughout his career, both as a cop and an undercover detective.

She leaned towards Mel and whispered, "Why are they asking him these questions? It has nothing to do with the salon."

Mel put her arm around her and placed her mouth at Charlotte's ear. "He's trying to discredit Ren in front of the jury by questioning all of the decisions he's made in his career. It's the same technique he used on you. Only yours was on a more personal level."

She hesitated. "As awful as it is, it's a good sign. The defense is grasping at straws, looking for anything that will make his clients look less terrible in the eyes of the jury."

"Detective Flynn, we've heard testimony today that my

client forced you to take Ms. Montgomery into the back room of the salon and have sex with her. Is this correct?"

"Yes." Ren's gaze landed on Charlotte for the first time since he had entered the courtroom. His grey eyes stared into hers, and she started to shake. Mel squeezed her shoulder and pulled her a little closer.

"You had sex with her because Mr. Terrence allegedly threatened to kill both Officer Shallen and Ms. Montgomery if you didn't. Is this correct?"

"Yes."

"Is it true that you knew Officer Shallen before the incident in the salon?"

Ren nodded. "Yes."

"How long have you known him?" the defense attorney asked.

"Twenty years, give or take."

"Would you consider him a friend?"

"Yes."

"And yet when my client allegedly threatened Officer Shallen's life, you said, and I quote, 'What the hell do I care about the life of some cop? Go ahead and kill him.' Is this correct?"

"Yes," Ren said.

The defense attorney smoothed his tie. "Just one last question, Detective Flynn. Is it true that two days after the incident at the salon, Officer Shallen reported to your supervisors that you had raped Ms. Montgomery, and subsequently, you were charged with rape?"

There was another collective gasp through the courtroom. Charlotte leaned forward, looking past Mel to stare in horror at Vince. He was staring down at the floor between his feet, his face pale and sick looking.

Ren cleared his throat. "Yes, but -"

"And is it true that two of the three salon employees, Miss

Darlene Smith and Mrs. Rita Tanden, both supported Officer Shallen's accusation of rape?"

"Yes, but they weren't in the back room with us. They made an assumption and -"

"Thank you, Detective Flynn. I have no further questions." The defense attorney returned to his seat as the judge looked at Michael.

"Cross-examine, Mr. Winters?"

"Yes, thank you, your honour. Detective Flynn, would you have let Mr. Terrence kill Officer Shallen?"

"No."

"Even if it had blown your cover?" Michael said.

"I wouldn't have let Vince die. I was bluffing. If Char – if Ms. Montgomery hadn't stepped forward and said she would play his game, I would have figured out a way to stop Steve from killing Vince," Ren said.

"The rape charges against you were dropped only a day later. Is this correct?" Michael said.

"Yes. Ms. Montgomery woke from her surgery and, after being questioned by Vince, confirmed that the sex between us was consensual. Vince immediately phoned my supervisors and told them of his mistake. They then questioned Ms. Montgomery themselves, and she also told them that the sex had been consensual. They dropped the charges after that."

Charlotte cupped her elbows. The day after she told Vince that Ren hadn't raped her, two plain-clothes detectives had shown up in her hospital room and questioned her about the events in the salon. They had asked her bluntly if Ren had raped her, and although she was utterly mortified, she told them the truth. At the time, she hadn't thought much about their questioning and assumed they were involved in the investigation at the salon.

"Ms. Montgomery testified that after you had intercourse

with her, you gave her your gun as protection against Mr. Terrence. Is this true?"

Ren nodded. "Yes."

"Why didn't you just use the gun to kill Mr. Terrence?"

"Because my orders were to bring Steve in alive. My supervisors were very specific about that. It's why I shot him in the side instead of the head." There was more than a hint of disgust in Ren's voice.

"And yet, you gave Ms. Montgomery your gun and told her to shoot Mr. Terrence if he tried to harm her," Michael said. "Why?"

Ren frowned. "Because Steve was high on coke. He was acting irrationally and crazy and had already indicated he wanted Ms. Montgomery. I had lived with the man at the clubhouse for nearly a year. I knew exactly what he was capable of. I didn't care what my supervisors wanted. I wasn't about to let an innocent woman be raped or killed."

"Thank you, Detective Flynn. I have no further questions." Michael returned to his seat as Ren nodded and left the witness box. He walked through the gate that separated the viewing area from the rest of the courtroom. He sat in the row behind Charlotte, and she fancied she could almost feel his eyes burning into her skull.

She stared at the floor, concentrating on her breathing and barely hearing the conversation between the judge and lawyers. She clenched her hands and desperately listened for the judge to dismiss them. After nearly ten minutes, he did, and she shot to her feet and broke for the door, refusing to look at Ren as she passed him.

"Charlotte, wait!" Vince shouted, but she ignored him. She fled the courthouse, pushing past the waiting reporters and running for her car. She climbed in and drove off, her heart beating frantically in her chest and her breath coming in harsh, hot gasps.

# CHAPTER 6

Charlotte peered through the peep hole and sighed. Vince, twisting his hands nervously, was standing on her doorstep. It had been two days since she had testified in court, and she had holed up in her house, calling in sick to work and refusing to answer her phone.

"Please, Charlotte. I know you're in there," Vince called through the door.

"Go away, Vince," Charlotte said.

"Just let me in so I can explain. Please. I'm not leaving until you do."

"Goddammit." She waited another minute and then yanked the door open. "You have five minutes."

He followed her into the house and down the hallway to the kitchen. He sat at the table as she leaned against the counter and glared at him.

"Well? I'm waiting," she said.

"I couldn't tell you that I knew Ren. I couldn't risk blowing his cover, Charlotte. I'm sorry."

She snorted. "Blow his cover? He just testified in the

largest kidnapping and drug trafficking trial our town has ever seen. I think his cover is blown."

Vince sighed. "Until a week ago, Ren had no plan to testify. Michael felt that we had enough evidence without Ren's testimony. He could stay 'dead' and continue his work as an undercover detective."

"So why did he testify?"

"Ren decided he didn't want to be in undercover work anymore." He frowned and stared at the cap in his hands. "To say his supervisors were surprised is an understatement. He's very good at what he does."

"Why didn't you tell me then?"

"I wanted to. Michael and Ren asked me not to. Michael was worried it would affect how you testified, and Ren thought it would be best not to spring it on you right before your testimony."

"Bullshit," Charlotte said. "Knowing he was alive and a detective wouldn't have changed my testimony. I didn't know who he was when I screwed him in the back of the salon, and I would have said as much at the trial."

Vince winced. "Charlotte, I'm so -"

"Save it, Vince. You've already apologized a million times, and I've repeatedly told you that it wasn't your fault. I don't want to talk about it anymore. Besides, thanks to the defense attorney, you and half the goddamn town know just how much I enjoyed the little tryst with Ren."

She dropped into a chair and lowered her head onto the table. "God, I've never been so embarrassed in my life."

Vince patted her arm gingerly. "It'll all work out, Charlotte."

She cocked her head to the right, feeling the coolness of the wood under her burning cheek, and rolled her eyes at him. "Of course it will. I mean, yeah, Helen tells every single person who walks into the salon about what a slut I am and how I screwed a gang member three months after my poor, sick husband died. Oh, and she delights in giving them all the dirty details, like how they could hear me moaning and the dryer hitting the wall as we had sex. But I'm sure in the last ten months, no one has been calling me the town whore behind my back."

Vince's cheeks were so red with embarrassment that Charlotte would have laughed if she hadn't been so angry.

"Charlotte, everyone knows that Helen is a mean old gossip. No one believes what she says, and -"

"Except two days ago, I confirmed it under oath, remember?"

"Yeah, I remember. But now that people know Ren wasn't a criminal, that he was a detective, maybe -"

She threw her hands up in the air. "Well, hallelujah! Charlotte Montgomery isn't a criminal-banging slut. She's just a slut! Thank you, Vince. My reputation is safe once more."

Vince's face crumpled, and for one horrifying moment, she thought he was going to cry. Her heart twisted in her chest. Vince and his family were the closest thing she had to family since Rick died, and she was suddenly deeply ashamed of her behaviour. He hadn't wanted to lie to her, and she knew that no matter what she said to him, he would always blame himself for what happened in the salon that day.

"Vince." She straightened before reaching across the table and squeezing his hands. "I'm sorry. I shouldn't have said that. I know you couldn't tell me about Ren and didn't mean to hurt me. I'm just shocked and embarrassed and – hell, I don't know - the whole situation is just screwed up."

He stared miserably at her, and she gave him a small smile. "It just means a few more years of therapy, that's all. My therapist will probably send you a fruit basket in thanks."

His lips twitched slightly, and she squeezed his hands again before releasing them. "Vince?"

"Yeah?"

"Ren said you two were friends. Were you?"

Vince nodded. "Yes. I was actually very good friends with Ren's father. He died when Ren was still in his mid-teens, and Mel and I took him under our wing."

Charlotte frowned. "How could I have not met him before? Rick and I were at your place plenty of times for barbecues and parties."

"He moved away before we even met you and Rick. We've kept in touch with Ren mostly through email and phone calls. Then he went into undercover work, and we lost track of him for a few years."

"Why would he come back to the town he grew up in to work undercover?" Charlotte said.

"I don't think he had much choice. He was trying to bring down Steve's club, and Steve moved them from Branston to our town about six months ago. It was go with him or blow his cover, I suppose."

He paused. "Besides, I doubt anyone would recognize Ren. He looks completely different. Hell, I hardly recognized him." He stared down at his hands for a moment.

"Why did you tell his supervisors that he raped me? You – you were friends with him." Charlotte's voice was so low he almost didn't hear the question.

He looked up at her, and this time, his eyes were swimming with tears. "Because I thought he did. He had been undercover for a long time, which sometimes changes people. Even good cops – *good men* – like Ren."

He wiped at the tears that were starting to slide down his cheeks. "You went back there with him willingly. You played Steve's sick, awful game to save my life, and in return had to – to..."

He took a deep breath. "I didn't want Ren to get away

with it, even if he was my friend, just because you said you would go back there with him."

"Oh, Vince," Charlotte said. "Honey, I've told you this before, but it was consensual. Ren didn't hurt or force me."

She gave him a small smile. "You were too busy bleeding to death to pay much attention, but hell, ask Helen. She'll give you all the dirty details."

He didn't laugh at her small joke. "When you woke up and told me it was consensual and how Ren gave you his gun for protection, I thought I was going to vomit. I immediately called Ren's supervisors, and they dropped the charges quickly, but Ren was already angry and upset. He hasn't spoken to me since that day."

He studied the table between them. "I've fucked everything up so badly, Charlotte. I got myself shot, I nearly got you killed, I accused my friend of rape, and I lied to you. Now, you and Ren hate me, and I don't know how to get either of you to forgive me. I've made such a mess of things."

"I don't hate you, Vince. And I forgive you for lying to me," Charlotte said.

He pulled a handkerchief out of his pocket and wiped his cheeks before blowing his nose. "That means a lot to me, Charlotte."

She smiled and reached out to squeeze his hand again. "I love you, Vince."

He blushed a little. "I love you too, Charlotte. Both Mel and I do."

He stood up. "I should get home to Mel. The defense wrapped up their case today, and they did closing arguments. The jury is deliberating. Michael says it won't be long. He thinks they'll have their decision by tomorrow, and it'll be guilty. Steve and Jasper, as well as the other club members, will go to prison for life based on your and the other ladies' testimonies and based on the evidence that Ren has collected over the last year."

"That's good." Charlotte walked him to the door and kissed his cheek as he stepped onto the porch.

"Will you come for a barbeque this weekend?" Vince asked. "Mel is thinking of inviting Michael and a few other people."

She nodded. "I'll be there."

# CHAPTER 7

Charlotte took a deep breath and squeezed Mel's hand. They were in the courtroom waiting to hear the verdict, and although she was confident that the jury would find Steve and Jasper guilty, she couldn't stop her stomach from rolling and twisting with nausea.

For what felt like the fiftieth time, she started to stare at Ren, who was sitting a few rows back and forced herself to stop. For a few months after the incident at the salon, she'd had nightmares. Nightmares where Vince had died as she watched helplessly, or nightmares where she was shot in the head instead of her shoulder. She would wake shuddering and gasping, her body covered in sweat and tears sliding down her cheeks. They stopped eventually, and she had been grateful. But last night, she'd returned to the salon in her dreams again.

Her cheeks flushed. It hadn't been a nightmare. This time, she was in the back room of the salon, sitting on the dryer with Ren between her legs. They were naked, and there was no worry or sense of urgency this time. He spent long minutes touching and caressing her until she was moaning.

She'd kissed him eagerly, pressing against him when he slid his cock into her. She'd traced his chest tattoos with her fingertips as he moved within her in a hard, deep rhythm.

She woke before he could bring her to orgasm. Her heart was beating frantically in her chest, and her pelvis was throbbing and aching. She'd pushed a trembling hand between her legs, not surprised to feel the moisture that had collected there. She brought herself to a quick but oddly unsatisfying climax and tried not to dwell too much on the fact that at the moment of her climax, Ren's face popped into her mind.

The judge entered the courtroom, and she stood with the others as he sat down. He motioned for them to be seated, and Charlotte squeezed Mel's hand again, her heart racing in her chest.

* * *

"ORDER! ORDER IN THE COURT!" THE JUDGE BANGED HIS gavel and glared around the courtroom. The jury had just delivered their guilty verdict, and the courtroom had erupted with noise.

Charlotte grinned at Mel and Vince as the bailiffs led Jasper and Steve from the courtroom. Steve whipped around as they moved them toward the far door and glared at Vince and Charlotte.

"I'll kill all of you. Do you hear me?" Steve screamed, spittle flying from his mouth. His hot glare moved to Darlene, Rita, and Helen, standing wide-eyed in the row across from Vince and Charlotte.

He shifted his gaze to Charlotte and grinned at her, his eyes glowing with madness. "You're going to regret the day you met me, bitch."

Charlotte stepped back, her breath catching in her throat

as fear speared its way through her chest. She wanted to be brave, didn't want to show the asshole that he was frightening her, but her entire body was trembling, and she was more scared now than she had been in the salon.

The bailiff started to drag him away, and suddenly Ren was standing in front of her, and Steve was shouting at him. "You're dead, you son of a bitch! You and your skinny little bitch!"

He was dragged from the room, and Charlotte took another step back. Ren turned and lightly gripped her upper arms.

"Are you okay?" His deep voice washed over her, and she stared up at him mutely. She was struck with the sudden urge to put her arms around his waist and bury her head in his chest. He would be warm, she remembered how warm he was, and as long as she was in his arms, nothing bad could happen to her. She swayed towards him when her common sense kicked in, and she freed herself.

"I'm fine," she said.

Vince squeezed past Mel and rested his hand on her back. Ren looked away, his tanned face expressionless.

"Charlotte? Are you okay?" Vince said.

"I'm *fine*." She shrugged off his hand. She wasn't fine. Steve screaming that he would kill her had shaken her badly, but she wasn't sure if it was that or Ren's large body that was sucking the oxygen from the room.

She staggered away. "I just need some fresh air."

"Charlotte – wait."

She ignored Vince and pushed her way through the crowd towards the door. She opened it and threw her hand before her face as the reporters crowded around her. The cameras nearly blinded her, and she staggered back as microphones were shoved in front of her face.

"Ms. Montgomery! How do you feel about today's verdict?"

"Ms. Montgomery! Have you spoken with Detective Flynn since discovering he was an undercover detective?"

"No comment!" she shouted and pushed her way past them. They followed her, still shouting their questions, and she broke into a run and bolted down the hallway. She turned left. This hallway was blessedly quiet, and she made a beeline for the first door she saw. Praying it was an empty room, she turned the door handle and slipped inside, shutting the door behind her.

"Nice," she groaned.

She was in a broom closet. The smell of cleaning fluids assaulted her nostrils, and she muttered a curse as she tripped over a mop and crashed into the wall. It was completely dark, the only light was a thin strip coming from the bottom of the door, and she stumbled over the bucket that accompanied the mop before giving up and leaning against the wall.

She could feel her heart thudding in her ears, and she closed her eyes and began to count backwards from a hundred. When she got to zero, she opened her eyes. They had adjusted to the dark, and she could see the large wire shelf on the opposite side of the small room. It was filled with bottles, and she stared blankly at them as she tried to decide what to do.

"C'mon, Charlotte. You can't stay in here forever," she said.

She was reaching for the door handle when the door opened. She blinked at the sudden blinding light and just had time to recognize Ren's face before he was in the closet with her and shutting the door behind him. They were plunged into darkness again, and she took a nervous step back. The closet was small, and Ren was too large and too close.

"Ms. Montgomery."

"Detective."

"How are you?"

"Great. How are you? You look pretty good for a dead man."

She felt more than saw him wince, and he sighed deeply but didn't answer. He continued to stay silent, and she wanted to speak and fill the space between them in nervous chatter, but she clamped her lips shut and waited.

"Ms. Montgomery?"

"Yes, Detective?"

"You know you're in a broom closet, right?"

"I do. How did *you* know I was in a broom closet?"

"I'm a detective. It's what I do."

She almost snorted laughter and threw her hand over her mouth to stifle it. She didn't want Ren to make her laugh. She didn't want to like him and most certainly didn't want to wonder what he would do if she stepped closer and pressed her mouth against his.

It was warm in the broom closet, and she could feel sweat trickling down her back, dampening her blouse under her jacket. She was horrified to realize that her nipples had hardened, and her core was aching and pulsing.

*It's because of your sex dream last night,* she told herself. *Now you're stuffed in this closet with him, and he's tall and handsome and saved your life, and you know what it's like to have him inside you, for God's sake. What you're feeling is perfectly normal.*

She shut her eyes. She had no idea if what she was feeling was normal. She'd have to ask her therapist.

"Ms. Montgomery?"

"Yes, Detective?"

"Why are you in a broom closet?"

"I have a secret identity."

"I'm sorry?"

61

"I have a secret identity, and you've stumbled on it. Would you like to know who I really am?"

"Yes."

She took a step closer until her breasts were nearly brushing against his chest. He leaned down, and she put her mouth to his ear. "Are you sure, Detective?"

He tried to speak and produced nothing but a low groan. He cleared his throat and tried again. "Yes. Who are you?"

"I'm Batman," she whispered in a deep and throaty voice.

He jerked back in surprise, his ass hitting the shelf behind him, and cursed softly as cleaning products fell off the top shelf and landed on his head. She smothered a giggle as he rubbed the top of his skull.

"You've found the entrance to the Bat Cave. Well done, Detective. You've earned another Boy Scout badge."

He surprised her by chuckling. "You're funny. I wasn't expecting that."

"So glad I could surprise you," she said. She tried to shift backwards subtly. When she had whispered in Ren's ear, she had almost sucked his earlobe into her mouth. Jesus. She was going crazy.

"So, how long are you planning on staying in the broom closet, Ms. Montgomery?"

"Until the reporters are gone." She leaned against the wall and waited for him to leave, ignoring the part of her that hoped he would stay.

\* \* \*

REN NEEDED TO LEAVE THE CLOSET. SHE WANTED HIM TO leave, but he couldn't seem to do it.

"I don't need a babysitter, Detective," Charlotte said.

"I've been worried about you. I've wondered how you've been the last ten months," he said.

It was the understatement of the year. For the last ten months, he had thought of nothing but her.

"Oh, you know – can't complain. I spent three months in physical therapy, re-learning how to use my arm after being shot in the shoulder by an asshole. The good news is I can now proudly raise my left arm to wave at people again. The bad news is no one waves at me anymore. Oh, and let's not forget how I spent six months being repeatedly tested to make sure I hadn't picked up an STI after having unprotected sex with a tattooed biker who was holding me hostage. Thank God I'm on the pill and didn't have to worry about getting pregnant."

"Ms. Montgomery, I -"

She talked over him. "And then there's my new reputation as the town whore. That's been lots of fun. You missed it, but you should have seen the lookie-loo's faces in the courtroom when I admitted to having an orgasm while fucking you. I swear to God, the judge allowed the question just because *he* wanted to know. That juicy tidbit will give the good folks of this town something to talk about for *years*."

"Ms. Montgomery -"

"Oh, for Pete's sake!" she snapped. "You've been *inside* me, Ren. I think we're past Ms. Montgomery, don't you?"

"I'm sorry, Charlotte."

Ren was acutely aware of Charlotte's soft breathing and how her faint floral scent filled the broom closet. It was a scent that he had only smelled in his dreams for the last ten months, and he was intoxicated by both it and the closeness of her body.

"Why didn't you tell me who you were when we were in the back room together?" she said.

"It would have put you in more danger. Plus, I couldn't risk having you blow my cover. I'd been with Steve's club for over a year, and we were close to busting them. Besides, I didn't think it would make a difference."

"Wouldn't make a difference?" He could hear the anger in her voice. "I spent the last ten months thinking I'd had sex with a gang member. Thinking that I'd betrayed my husband's memory with a criminal who probably had sex with every woman who opened her legs to him. Thinking that I was a – a whore for enjoying it when you fucked me!"

Her voice was rising, and he gently rubbed her arm. "Charlotte -"

"Don't touch me!" She yanked away from him, her voice full of venom. "Do you have any idea how that made me feel? I've spent countless hours trying to understand what was wrong with me that I would enjoy having sex with a man, a criminal, that I had just met. That I would just – just forget that I was a hostage, that my friend was dying, that my husband had died only three months before. Normal people don't do that, Ren!"

He grunted in surprise when she pushed herself away from the wall and hammered his chest with her small fists. He barely felt the blows, but when she whimpered, "I hate you," he winced as though she had stabbed him with a knife.

"I'm so sorry."

"I hate you!" She said it louder, and when she tried to punch him in the face, he wrapped his arms around her, pinning her arms to her side, and held her against his broad chest.

"Let go of me, you asshole!" She squirmed and writhed for a few minutes, kicking at his shins with her feet before collapsing weakly against him and beginning to cry. He released her cautiously and was surprised when she put her arms around his waist instead of moving away and buried her face in his chest.

"I really, really hate you," she mumbled into his suit jacket.

"I know." His hands itched to stroke her soft blonde hair, and he gave in to the temptation and threaded his fingers through it. She twitched in surprise but didn't move away.

"You have every right to hate me, and I'm so sorry." He rubbed her back with long, slow strokes. She fit in his arms perfectly, he mused, like she was meant to be there. "Tell me what I can do to make it up to you. I'll do whatever you ask."

She was quiet for a few seconds and said, "Forgive Vince."

He stiffened. "I can't do that."

With a soft sigh, she pushed away from his embrace and leaned against the wall again. His eyes had adjusted to the dim light, and he could see the frown on her face. "You said whatever I asked. I'm asking you to forgive Vince."

"He accused me of raping you." His voice was thick with hurt.

"Can you blame him? He was shot, barely conscious,s and had lost a lot of blood. He didn't know what happened between us in the back room."

"He knew me. We were friends. He knew who I was, and for him to think that I would hurt you..."

"He thought you might have changed. He hadn't seen you in years – how was he to know?"

"He should have," he said.

"Well, he didn't, and you can't blame him for that. He was trying to protect me, trying to atone for a situation he thought was his fault. He feels terrible about what happened – it's eating him up inside. He's a good man, and he doesn't deserve this."

"He could have asked me. He could have -"

"The minute he found out that the sex was consensual, he went to your supervisors and admitted his mistake. Ren, you asked me what you could do to make up for that day in the salon. I'm telling you. Are you going to do it or not?"

"I'll try," he said.

"Good."

He shifted a little closer to her. "Why didn't you tell them it was rape, Charlotte? I was dead. There would be no one to argue your story, and it would have saved your reputation."

"I couldn't do something like that. I couldn't lie about what had happened. No matter how it made me feel about myself or the type of person it made me, I couldn't say it was rape when it wasn't."

She pushed her hair back from her face. "Besides, as Helen has pointed out to every single one of her clients, the moaning I was doing in the back room indicated quite strongly that I was enjoying myself."

Her words sent a shiver down his spine. Even after nearly a year, he could easily remember the sound of her moaning. The way she had reacted to his touch and how warm and wet and tight she was had been the subject of his fantasies for the last ten months.

The tiny broom closet suddenly seemed even tinier, claustrophobic almost, and he could feel sweat breaking out on his forehead. He wanted to kiss her, wanted to find out if she tasted as good as he remembered in his dreams, but she hated him. He had to face the fact that his dreams were the only place he would touch her now.

"Ren?"

"Yeah?" He stepped back and stumbled into the wire shelving behind him. More cleaning products tumbled from the shelf, and a can of something heavy landed on his foot with a painful thud.

"Dammit."

"What's wrong?" She reached out in the darkness, her fingers brushing his mouth, and he inhaled sharply.

"Ren?" He could hear the concern in her voice as she moved closer. He tried desperately to move away, but he was trapped between the shelf and her small body.

"Are you hurt?" Her fingers traced his jaw line and then his cheekbone before she pressed her hand against his forehead.

"Jesus, you're really warm," she said.

"I'm fine." He twisted his head to escape her touch, gasping again when she cupped his face in her hands.

"Maybe you have the flu. You're trembling."

He curled his hands into fists to stop himself from yanking her against him. His cock was hard and throbbing in his pants, and he couldn't stop thinking about the day in the salon. How warm she had been, how soft, eager, and willing she was for his touch.

"You should stop touching me now, Charlotte," he said.

Her hands tightened briefly on his face as her breath quickened, and he inhaled deeply. She was suddenly aware of how much he wanted her, he was certain of it, and he groaned inwardly.

"You should go," he nearly pleaded.

Instead of leaving, she took a hesitant step forward until her small breasts brushed against his chest. It was all the invitation he needed. His hands shot out, and he grabbed her hips and snatched her against him. She had time for a tiny squeak of surprise before his mouth was on hers, and his tongue pushed hungrily past her lips.

* * *

CHARLOTTE MOANED INTO REN'S MOUTH. WHAT THEY WERE doing was a mistake. She knew it was wrong, but that knowledge didn't stop her from throwing her arms around his neck and pressing herself eagerly against him.

His hands - his warm and deliciously hard hands - were pushing her jacket from her body while his tongue continued to taste and lick and skate across her own. She closed her lips around his tongue and sucked hard, pulling a groan of desire from his throat.

She moved her hands to his jacket, tugging at the buttons until his jacket opened, and she could slide it from his broad shoulders. It joined hers on the floor, and she yanked at his tie and unbuttoned his dress shirt as his trembling fingers unbuttoned hers. He nearly ripped her shirt open, his large hands cupping her breasts through her bra with warm familiarity.

She traced his naked chest with her fingertips, rubbing the coarse hair between her fingers before tweaking one flat nipple. He twitched, his breath exploding from his throat in a long, hoarse moan as she kissed her way down his throat. She bit his collarbone and then moved back up his neck to his ear, sucking the lobe into her mouth like she had wanted to do earlier.

"Oh my God, Charlotte," he muttered. He grabbed her ass and pulled her against him. She could feel his erection pushing against her belly, and she wiggled her hand between them and cupped it through his pants.

He growled, the sound sending shivers down her spine, and then his hands cupped her thighs under her skirt, and he lifted her and shoved her back against the wall.

"Put your legs around me," he demanded.

She hooked her legs around his hips as he pressed her hard against the wall and rubbed his erection against her throbbing pussy. She moaned, her back arching, as he supported her weight with his lower body and pulled the cups of her bra down. Her small breasts spilled out, and he dipped his head and sucked a nipple into his mouth. His tongue swept across the sensitive tip, abrading it with long, slow strokes that had her panting with pleasure.

She threaded her fingers through his hair and clutched his head to her breast as he nipped lightly at the nipple before kissing across her chest to the other. He gave it the same treatment, running his tongue repeatedly over her nipple until it had tightened into a hard pink bud in his mouth.

"Ren," she moaned, and he kissed her again. Their tongues tangled together in a haze of need and want and lust, and she thrust her pelvis frantically against him. She didn't protest when he slipped his hand under her skirt. He traced the smooth skin of her inner thigh before stroking her through the material of her panties, and she moaned her need.

He pushed the crotch of her panties to the side, his breath harsh and hot in her ear, and then his fingers were pushing into her, and he could feel how wet and ready she was for him.

She was reaching for his belt buckle when the door to the broom closet flung open, and bright light flooded in. The janitor stared at them in shock as Ren automatically leaned forward, shielding her naked breasts from his view.

"I... I need a broom." The janitor, the tag on his shirt said Albert, reached in and grabbed the large broom leaning on the wall beside them. He slammed the door shut, plunging them into darkness once more.

"Oh, sweet Jesus!" Charlotte pushed roughly at Ren. "What the hell am I doing? Let me go!"

Ren dropped her gently to the floor and eased away from her. She tucked her breasts back into her bra and quickly buttoned her shirt as he buttoned his own. She reached down and snagged her jacket from the floor, shoving her arms into it.

"Charlotte, I'm sorry. I shouldn't have done that. I don't know what -"

She held up her hand. "Stop, Ren. Please. My life was threatened, reporters are hounding me, and then I lost my mind entirely and nearly had sex with you in a goddamn broom closet. Oh - and I gave Albert the janitor a free show of my tits. Don't take this the wrong way, but I really need to get away from you."

She ripped open the door and hurried out of the closet. Albert the janitor was nowhere in sight, and Charlotte hurried around the corner, not waiting to see if Ren was following her.

"Charlotte! Where have you been?"

Mel, Michael, and Vince were standing in the courthouse foyer. The reporters were gone, and she heaved a sigh of relief.

"I went to the washroom," she said.

"Are you feeling okay? You look flushed," Mel said.

"I feel fine."

Mel's eyes flickered to her left. "Hello, Ren."

"Hi, Mel."

After a brief hesitation, Mel stepped toward him and hugged him. "It's good to see you again."

They stood in awkward silence for a moment, and Charlotte looked at Ren pointedly.

He cleared his throat. "Hello, Vince."

Vince gave him a startled look. "Hey, Ren."

After another moment of awkwardness, Michael smiled at Charlotte. "Are you ready for that drink now?"

"What?" Ren was standing distractingly close to her, and she forced herself to focus on Michael.

"A drink. Remember, I promised you one after all this was done."

"Right, of course."

"Shall we go?"

He held his arm out to her. After a brief hesitation, she took it. "Yes, I'd like that."

She was lying. What she wanted was to take Ren home,

lead him into her bedroom, strip off his clothes, and ride him to a body-shuddering orgasm.

"Great! Vince, Mel – I'll talk to you later. Detective." Michael smiled at them and led Charlotte towards the door.

She glanced over her shoulder at Ren. He stared at them, his face an expressionless mask, but his hands were rolled into tight fists. She quickly turned around and followed Michael into the warm sunshine.

# CHAPTER 8

Charlotte parked her car in the driveway of Vince and Mel's modest bungalow and stepped from the vehicle. She reached under her shorts and tugged self-consciously at her bathing suit bottom before heading around to the side of the house.

It was Saturday afternoon. Mel had reminded her last night about the barbeque, and she'd been this close to begging off. It had been a hell of a few days. Work was busy, although she suspected that it was because people wanted to come in and gawk at her more than because they needed a haircut, and she hadn't slept well since the day in the courtroom. Her dreams were filled with images of Ren and his hard body, and she kept waking from her fitful bouts of sleep, feeling an odd mixture of confusion and horniness.

When she started to decline the party, Mel cut her off before she could really get started. "You're coming, Charlotte. This is a celebration of the nightmare finally being over, and you need to be there. It will mean a lot to Vince."

She opened the gate and walked down the narrow stone pathway between the fence and the house. She could hear laughter and the low murmur of talking as she entered the spacious backyard enclosed with a cedar fence. On her far left was the in-ground pool they had installed over four years ago. To her right was a large stone patio with a barbeque. Chairs and tables dotted the small grassy area behind the patio, and she could see Mel and Daniel and six or seven of Vince's work colleagues.

There was a shrill squeal beside her, and she turned to see Jade standing there. The young woman wore a tiny bikini, and her short dark hair was wet and spiky.

"Charlotte! I'm so glad to see you!" She hugged Charlotte enthusiastically.

"It's good to see you too, honey." She stepped back and stared at the young woman. "You're looking fantastic."

"Thanks! Dad hates this bathing suit. He forbids me to wear it, but I'm nearly twenty-one – his days of forbidding are long over." Jade grinned at her.

"Are you home for the summer?"

"Yup. I got home two weeks ago. I've been taking a bit of a holiday, but now I need to start looking for a job." She grinned impishly at Charlotte. "I've already had both Tony and Stan offer to get me a job at the station."

"I bet you have." Charlotte rolled her eyes as Jade snickered.

"Yeah, I turned them down. I don't think I want to work that closely with Dad. Now that I've had a taste of parental freedom, it's kind of hard to go back, you know?"

Mel appeared beside them, giving Charlotte a one-armed hug before staring affectionately at her daughter. "Hey, Jade? Do you think if you tried a little harder, you could find a bathing suit that lets even more of your ass hang out?"

Jade laughed and wiggled her butt at her mother before sauntering back to the pool.

Mel shook her head and smiled at Charlotte. "I'm thrilled you came, honey."

"Me too."

"How was your drink with Michael?" Mel said.

"It was good. We weren't out for long. Just had a drink, and then I headed home."

"That was it?"

"Well, we talked about some personal stuff. Did you know Michael was the youngest lawyer in forty years to be offered a position at Richardson and Company?"

"Vince told me."

"He turned them down. He said he couldn't picture himself defending sleazeballs like Steve for the next thirty years. I admire that."

Mel smiled at her. "It sounds like you had a good time."

"We did."

"He was happy to hear you would be joining us today." She pointed toward the pool. Michael was sitting on the edge of it, his feet and legs dangling in the water as he spoke with Daniel. His blond hair glowed in the afternoon light, and his short, muscular body was tanned from the sun.

"Was he?" A bad feeling developed in the pit of Charlotte's stomach.

"Definitely," Mel said.

It was an excellent time to change the subject. "What can I do to help?"

"You don't have to help, sweetie. Just sit and relax. Why don't you go and visit with Michael?"

"Nope. I'm helping, or I'm going home. You don't need to do all of the work."

Mel hesitated. "Well, if you wouldn't mind going into the kitchen and grabbing the potato salad and the green salad from the fridge, I would appreciate it."

"Of course." Charlotte headed into the house. It was

stupid of her not to realize that Michael wanted to be more than friends.

*Not that stupid. You dated Rick for two years and were married for six. You haven't been hit on in eight years. It's not surprising you didn't recognize the flirting. Besides, you don't think of Michael as anything more than a friend.*

As she closed the patio door and headed down the hallway towards the kitchen, she wondered if that was true. Yes, she decided. Michael was good looking, clever, and funny, but she felt nothing more than friendship. Part of her tried to insist it was because she still felt like she was married to Rick and that it would betray him. She glanced down at her left hand. She had taken her wedding ring off nearly two months ago.

*It's not because you're worried you're betraying Rick,* a small, sly voice whispered in her head. *It's because of Ren. Michael's not attractive to you because you want Ren. Admit it, girl, you're thrilled he's alive and not just because he saved your life. You've been itching to get him into your bed since he walked into the courtroom. It doesn't matter that he's dangerous and utterly unlike anyone you ever imagined yourself being with. You had a taste of him ten months ago, and now you want more.*

She snorted in annoyance. Just two weeks ago, she thought she was ready to be done with therapy. Then Ren walked back into her life, and suddenly, she was considering upping her weekly therapy session to twice weekly.

Why did he have to be so nice? Why did he have to act like he cared for her and was truly upset about what had happened in the salon? He looked like a mean biker with his muscles and his tattoos. Why couldn't he be one? It would make it a lot easier to hate him. She stalked into the kitchen and yanked open the fridge door before bending and looking into it.

\* \* \*

FROM HIS SPOT ACROSS THE KITCHEN, REN SUCKED IN HIS breath when Charlotte bent in front of the open fridge. She wore a pale yellow tank top and jean shorts. Her bare legs were tanned and looked delectably smooth and touchable. Her shorts cupped her ass, the worn material straining against her skin. He wanted to walk across the room, run his hand over her ass, slip it between her legs and –

He reined in his imagination. He already had an erection, and it was embarrassingly noticeable in his swim trunks. Coming to the barbeque was a bad idea, but when Mel invited him, mentioning that both Charlotte and Michael would be there, he immediately said yes.

It was ridiculous to be jealous of the lawyer's obvious interest in Charlotte. She didn't belong to Ren and made it clear in the broom closet that she hated him. Of course, she had also made out with him and drove him nearly mad with need, but that didn't mean she liked him. Plenty of people had sex with someone they hated. Hell, his parents had been a prime example of that.

He pushed away from the counter. "Need some help?"

\* \* \*

CHARLOTTE REACHED FOR THE POTATO SALAD. AS HER FINGERS curled around the bowl, a deep voice said, "Need some help?"

She shrieked and bounced up, her head banging painfully into the top of the fridge.

"Son of a bitch!" She backed up, holding her head.

"Charlotte, I'm sorry. I didn't mean to startle you. Are you all right?" Ren joined her.

"Ren! You scared the hell out of me!" She smacked him lightly on the chest and realized just a moment too late that he was shirtless. As though it had a mind of its own, her hand flattened against his warm skin, and she traced the large skull tattoo on the right side of his chest.

"What are you doing here?" Her fingers continued to trace his tattoos.

"I'm doing what you asked – trying to forgive Vince. When they invited me, I figured you would like it if I said yes. Charlotte," he swallowed hard, "are you okay?"

"Yes." The throbbing in her head was probably still there, but the heat under her hand had completely obliterated it. "I like your tattoos."

Her left hand joined her right hand in tracing the tattoos that covered his broad chest. She ran her fingers across the name above his heart, secretly delighted by his quiet gasp. "Who's Esther?"

"My grandmother."

"You're close to her?"

"Yes."

She didn't resist when he let his hands rest on her hips. She traced the lion's head tattooed across his ribs. "This one must have hurt."

He shrugged. "A little."

He leaned back against the counter and tugged her closer. She came willingly enough, settling herself between his spread legs while she continued to run her hands over him. His erection was poking against her lower abdomen, and he moved his hands to her ass and cupped it through her shorts before pressing her more tightly against him. He rubbed and kneaded her ass as she examined the cross tattoo on his upper right arm and the pinup girl on his upper left.

"Did you get these tattoos after you joined Steve's gang?" Her voice was a little breathless, the only indication of the effect his hands had on her.

"Most of them before. There are a couple on my back that I got after."

"I've always wanted a tattoo," she said. "Something small and pretty like a daisy. It's my favourite flower."

"Why didn't you get one?"

He slipped his hands beneath her shorts and under her bikini bottom. He stroked and squeezed her bare skin. She arched her pelvis, just a little, but enough to make his cock rub against her stomach until he made a low groan.

"I don't know. I'm a little afraid of needles, and Rick never really cared for tattoos. He thought they were tacky and that nice girls didn't get them."

He bent his head and nuzzled his face into her neck. As his tongue traced a leisurely hot path across the sensitive skin, she arched her hips again.

"I find them sexy," she confessed and shivered delicately when his lips found her earlobe and sucked on it.

"I find you sexy," he whispered into her ear.

Her fingers went to the scar on the left side of his chest. No hair grew on it, and she rubbed it lightly before tracing the "Esther" tattoo again. "Did the bullet really get lodged in your lung?"

He nodded. "Yeah, but they got it out pretty easily. Your body slowed it down."

She leaned forward and placed a light kiss on the scar. "You saved my life that day."

"I got you shot. You almost died," he said.

She didn't reply, and he slipped his hands out of her shorts and grabbed the hem of her tank top. "Let me see yours."

He pulled the tank top over her head, setting it on the counter before staring at her.

Her scar was more prominent - an almost star-shaped patch of raised skin that went to the top of her perfect, pale shoulder and outward to just touch her collarbone. The skin on the scar was pink and shiny.

"Is it sore?" he said.

"No. I just don't scar very well," she said. "The doctors said it was Keloid scarring now."

She glanced down at it. "It doesn't hurt, but it's so ugly."

He shook his head. "It isn't. Everything about you is beautiful."

He moved her bathing suit strap off her shoulder and placed light kisses on the scarring. She moaned a little, her hands digging into his hard biceps.

He smiled down at her and kissed the tip of her nose. "You're so beautiful, Charlotte."

He traced the outline of her nipple that was clearly visible against the slippery dark blue material of her bikini.

"We probably shouldn't be doing this, Ren."

"I think we should." He hooked his hand around her thigh and lifted her leg, resting her knee against his hip. He stroked her leg and placed a smattering of gentle kisses across the top of her chest.

"In fact, it's all I've been thinking about for the last ten months." He traced her lower lip with his tongue. "The way you taste, the way you moan, how good it felt to be in you."

Charlotte's entire body was on fire with need. The way he was touching her right now, the way he repeatedly brushed his mouth against hers but pulled back whenever she tried to deepen the kiss, was driving her insane.

He stroked her back with light, delicate strokes. His touch was gentle, but she could sense the hunger and urgency underneath it. His hands paused at the clip to her bikini top, and he flicked it open before stroking her back again.

She could feel his surprise when she flattened herself against his chest and kissed him deeply. Her tongue flicked past his lips, and she explored his mouth with wet, hot licks until his gentleness was gone and his fingers were digging into her back.

"Charlotte, do you need -"

Charlotte tore her mouth from Ren's and looked behind her. Vince was standing in the doorway to the kitchen, and he looked horrified. Without speaking, he turned and left the kitchen.

"Goddammit! Vince – wait!" Charlotte started to go after him and scowled at Ren when he grabbed her arm. "Let go of me, Ren. I have to talk to him."

"Your bikini top," he said.

She looked down at herself and groaned. Her breasts were nearly falling out of her unclipped top. She reached behind her back and yanked at the straps. "Oh, for God's sake!"

He pushed her hands out of the way and clipped her top together for her. She covered her face for a moment, and he rested his hands on her shoulders. "Charlotte -"

"Nope," she said. "Do you know what I wish? I wish I could just once keep my clothes on when I'm around you. Does that seem like too much to ask? I don't think it is. Do you think it is?"

She could see him trying not to grin, and she gave him a fierce look of disapproval. "This is not funny, Ren."

"It's kind of funny."

"No, it isn't! I'm losing my mind. It's like – it's like you've cast some kind of spell on me."

"I haven't," Ren said. "I want you, and you want me. Why don't we say our goodbyes to the others and return to my place?"

"Are you crazy? I can't leave with you. What will the others say? I can't -"

She sucked in a huge gulp of oxygen. "Listen, Ren, near-death experience in a hostage situation aside, I'm not the type of girl who just falls into bed with someone she barely knows. I know I'm coming across that way, and I'm sorry. I don't mean to. I think we need to take a step back and -"

"I love you, Charlotte," Ren said.

Her eyes went wide, and she stepped back, picking nervously at the waistband of her jean shorts. "What?"

"I love you."

"You don't even know me."

"I know enough. I know I haven't been with anyone but you since that day in the salon. I know you're all I've thought about for nearly a year. I know that thinking of a life without you makes me feel lost. I know that I love you."

She punched him hard in the shoulder. "Stop saying that! You do not love me, Ren. Do you understand?"

She grabbed his shoulders and shook him when he didn't reply. "You have, like, I don't know, post-traumatic stress disorder or something. You can't be in love with me."

He shrugged. "I am."

"I leave my dirty underwear on the floor. I'm a terrible driver. I love reality television. I never vacuum, hate vegetables, and never return my library books on time."

He laughed. "That's adorable."

"It is not adorable," she said. "Seriously, I have terrible taste in television."

"Then I guess we'll have to find something else to do together instead of watching television." He gave her a slow and sexy grin.

Heat unfurled in her belly, and she squashed it down fiercely. Ren still stared calmly at her. She realized with amazement that she could see the love in his eyes. He did love her. Or at least thought he did.

Her heart opened to him for a moment, to the possibility

of accepting his love and loving him in return. It must have flickered in her eyes because his gaze widened, and he pulled her into his embrace.

He kissed her gently. "I know it's weird and strange and doesn't seem possible, but I love you, Charlotte."

She pushed away from him and picked up her shirt from the counter. She slipped it over her head. "We're too different, Ren. What you find exciting and new will eventually become stale and unappealing. We have nothing in common."

"Opposites attract, Charlotte."

"Only for a little while," she said. "I spend my weekends watching bad TV and going to the farmer's market. You'll get bored with me."

"I won't. Besides, you don't know me yet. Maybe those are the things I like too."

"Are they?"

He hesitated, and she shook her head. "You *will* get bored. Not to mention that I'm used to a certain type of man, and you -"

"Someone like Michael?" She could hear the jealousy in his voice.

"Michael's a nice man," she said.

"You don't want nice." His gaze dared her to deny it. "You want someone like me. Someone who excites you and wants you and loves you."

"Stop saying that!"

"Charlotte? Is everything all right?"

Michael stepped into the kitchen and stared at Ren. "Hello, Detective."

"Hey," Ren grunted.

Charlotte forced herself to smile at Michael. "Everything's fine. I was grabbing the salads for Mel." She tugged open the fridge door and pulled out both salads.

"Here, I'll help you." Michael took the potato salad from her.

"Thanks." She followed him out of the kitchen without looking at Ren.

# CHAPTER 9

Charlotte ate her ice cream cone and tried to ignore what felt suspiciously like jealousy growing in the pit of her stomach. After accepting her ice cream cone from Mel, Jade returned to sitting next to Ren on a small stone bench near the pool. The young woman giggled and flirted with him, patting his leg and resting her slender body against his arm.

She had been like this all evening. Charlotte couldn't blame her. Ren was hot. There was no point in denying it, and if she had been Jade's age, she would have been all over him as well and damn the age difference.

Ren was subtly edging away from Jade. Charlotte could see his gratitude when Mel brought him an ice cream cone and squeezed in between him and Jade on the bench. Jade frowned, and Mel grinned at her and lightly hip-checked her further down the bench.

"Charlotte?"

She looked up, her face reddening. "Hey, Vince."

"Hi, sweetie."

He sat in the lawn chair beside her, stretching out his legs and folding his hands in his lap. "Can we talk about what happened earlier?"

She looked around. Daniel floated in the pool while eating his ice cream cone, and Michael and the others gathered around the barbeque. Michael looked her way and waved, and she waved back.

"It wasn't what it looked like, Vince."

He didn't reply, and she sighed. "Shit. It was exactly what it looked like."

Vince snorted, and she glanced at him. She was shocked to see that he was trying to hide his laughter.

"This isn't funny, Vince."

"I know. I'm sorry. So, do you like him?"

"God, I don't know. I don't even know him. I find him attractive, but I don't know if that's because I'm lonely or if it's because he's so different from Rick, or -"

She had almost said, 'Because I'm really horny,' and she groaned inwardly and took another lick of her ice cream cone. She was close to Vince, but she wasn't that goddamn close.

"He's a good man, Charlotte."

"Yeah, I know."

Vince hesitated. "Did you ask him to forgive me?"

"I asked him to try. I told him that you did what you thought was right and that he needed to see it from your point of view."

"Thanks for that, honey. I really appreciate it."

He reached out his hand, and she squeezed it briefly.

"I meant it when I said he was a good guy. I know he looks a little rough around the edges, but we've been spending a lot of time together in the last two days, getting caught up, and he's the same Ren he was before," Vince said.

He glanced over at Ren before rolling his eyes. "Jade seems to be quite taken with him."

She laughed. "Watching him try to avoid her all night has been a little amusing."

"That girl of mine always did love the bad boys." He heaved a long-suffering sigh that made Charlotte laugh again.

"I thought you said Ren wasn't a bad boy?"

He grinned. "No, I said he was a good guy. There's a difference."

"Right."

A drip of ice cream slid down her hand, and she licked it away before taking another quick look at Ren. Jade leaned over her mother, chatting happily at him, but Ren stared across the pool at her. Even from here, she recognized the look in his eyes, and her lower body throbbed in silent response.

"So, are you two going to date?" Vince said.

She shrugged. "I don't think that's a good idea. There are already enough rumours going around about me. I don't need to add to them."

"Who cares what they say," Vince said. "People will gossip no matter what." He stared moodily across the yard. "You deserve to be happy, Charlotte."

"He says he loves me." She hadn't meant to say that.

Vince just nodded. "Yeah, I'm not surprised."

"What do you mean you're not surprised?" Charlotte said.

"He's been spending a lot of time at our place over the last two days, and all he talks about is you, Charlotte. He hasn't come right out and said it, but I'm pretty sure he left the undercover division because of you."

She sighed and tossed her empty cone into the small garbage can beside her before staring at Vince. "He's crazy, right?"

"No, I don't think so." He glanced at Mel. "I won't lie to you, Charlotte. Mel is pushing for something to happen with you and Michael. She thinks Ren is a great guy and cares about him like he's one of our own, but her overall feeling is that Michael would be better for you."

He gave her an appraising look. "Me, on the other hand? I'm rooting for Ren."

"Vince, he can't possibly be in love with me. He knows nothing about me. What he's feeling is lust and nothing more."

"Don't be so sure about that, Charlotte."

She rubbed her forehead. "I'm so tired, Vince. I don't even know what to think anymore. Rick's only been dead for a little over a year, and now I have both Michael and Ren interested in me, and I'm not even sure that I'm ready to date someone, let alone be in love again."

He squeezed her arm. "You should take a vacation, Charlotte. Get away from here for a while."

"Yeah, maybe I will."

She watched, her body tensing, as Ren stood and walked toward them. He stopped in front of them and smiled at Vince.

"Hey, Vince. Great barbeque – thank you for inviting me."

"I'm glad you could make it." Vince stood. "Here, take my seat. I'm going to go sit with Mel for a bit."

He left them, and Ren dropped into his seat.

"Hi, Charlotte."

"Hi, Ren."

"Are you okay?"

"Do you ever get tired of asking me if I'm okay?" she said.

He grinned. "Nope."

"I'm fine. I'm tired and will probably leave soon."

"Do you need a ride home? I've got my bike here, and I'd be happy to give you a lift."

"You have a motorcycle?" She didn't wait for him to answer. "Of course you have a motorcycle."

"So, do you need a lift home?"

She didn't reply. She had never been on a motorcycle in her life. She could imagine how it would feel, though. How it would feel to press against Ren's back, her thighs around his hips and her arms around his waist. He'd have a leather jacket, of course, and she could lay her cheek against its sun-kissed warmth, close her eyes, and just let him drive. She was surprised at how appealing that thought was to her. Until she met Ren, she never even pictured riding a motorcycle. Now, the idea sent tingles of excitement through her.

"Charlotte?"

"I drove my car here, but thank you."

"Would you like to have dinner with me tomorrow night?"

She sighed. "I don't think that's a good idea, Ren."

"But if Michael asks you, you'll accept," he said.

"No," she said. "I won't."

"I didn't mean to scare you earlier," he said.

"I know. It's just – it's a lot to take in."

He stared at his lap, and she said, "I just need some time, you know? To figure out things."

"I get it." He lifted his gaze to hers, his grey eyes filled with kindness and warmth. "I'll wait for you, Charlotte. I've waited ten months. I can wait longer."

# CHAPTER 10

C harlotte stepped out of her car and stretched, wincing slightly at the popping in her spine. The last two weeks had passed by in a blur. Michael had phoned her repeatedly after the party. After he showed up on her doorstep with flowers and a dinner invitation, she sat him down and explained that she wasn't interested in anything more than friendship.

She winced again as she walked toward her front door. The look of hurt on his face had been awful, but she hadn't wavered. She was lonely, and a part of her had enjoyed his phone calls and the attention, but she didn't feel anything for Michael but friendship. No matter how lonely she was, she wasn't about to lead him on.

Ren hadn't contacted her at all. She tried to tell herself that was a good thing, but on Wednesday night, when she had dinner with Vince and Mel, she couldn't stop from asking about him.

"He's fine," Vince said. "He asked for a transfer to our department, and it was granted. He's just trying to get back into the swing of living a normal life."

She rubbed the back of her neck as she climbed the stairs to her front porch. Work was crazy today. Helen hadn't shown up, and Darlene had left early to go to a concert with her boyfriend. She and Rita had been run off their feet, and neither had finished with clients until nearly seven.

She dug in her purse for her keys, squinting in the dim light. A storm was gathering. The sky had ominous looking black clouds, and distantly, she could hear the rumble of thunder. She muttered a curse under her breath, staring up at the light fixture just to the right of her door. The light bulb must have burnt out. She was sure she had left it on when she went to work this morning. Her fingers closed on the cold metal of her keys, and she grunted in satisfaction. She would have a hot bath and –

Strong fingers wrapped around her upper arm, and she was whirled around and shoved against the door of her house. Her keys fell to the porch floor, and her cry of surprise was cut short when a hand wrapped around her throat and squeezed, cutting off her air supply.

She stared in fear at the large man standing in front of her. She could see his scalp shining through his short and thinning grey hair. His eyes were so dark they looked black in the dim light, and his nose was permanently canted to the left.

"Hello, Charlotte." He grinned at her, revealing a mouthful of yellow teeth. "I've been waiting forever for you to get home."

She pulled at his hand, and he loosened his grip enough for her to take a ragged breath.

"No screaming now." He winked at her.

"Who are you?" she said.

"Oh, it don't matter who I am. All that matters is I give you the message he told me to give you."

"Who?" Tears slid down her cheeks.

"Why yer old friend Steve, that's who." The man grinned again and reached into his belt. He brought out a long and wickedly sharp knife, and she moaned with terror when he held it in front of her.

She started to struggle, and his hand closed brutally around her throat. She watched wide-eyed as he raised the knife high above his head.

"Steve says he'll see you in hell, Charlotte," the man said.

He was torn away from her before he could plunge the knife into her chest. She slumped against the door, watching with numb disbelief as the man tried to stab Ren standing behind him. Ren blocked the man's arm. Before the man could try to stab him again, Ren put his large hands around the man's head and twisted it sharply to the right.

The man collapsed to the porch. His eyes were open, and he had died with a mild look of surprise on his face. She watched as Ren dragged his body backward, hiding it in the shadows of her porch.

He picked up her keys and tugged her away from the door. She swayed alarmingly, and he braced her against his body before opening her front door and pulling her inside. He shut the door behind him and locked it.

"Charlotte, we need to go right now. You need to grab some stuff and come with me," he said.

She stumbled back from him. "You – you killed that man." She could feel hysteria bubbling up in her chest.

He nodded impatiently before peering down the dark hallway. "Yes, he was going to kill you. C'mon, Charlotte, we're wasting time."

He reached for her, his face twisting when she shrieked in fear and staggered away. Her back hit the wall, and a picture frame fell. It dropped to the floor, and the glass exploded with a jagged cough.

"Stay away from me." She held out her hands. They shook

violently, and she was hyperventilating. Her head buzzed, and Ren's voice was muffled and tinny sounding.

He held up his hands. "Honey, it's me. It's Ren. I love you, and I would never hurt you."

"Ren?" she whispered.

"Yes. You're okay, honey. Take some deep breaths."

"Okay. I'm okay," she repeated.

"Yes. I'm not going to -"

She suddenly threw herself at him and hugged him with panicky tightness. He put his arms around her and kissed her forehead, her cheeks and finally her mouth.

"What's happening, Ren?" she moaned.

"Steve's put a hit out on everyone that was in the salon that day." He hesitated. "Helen is dead, honey. I'm sorry. Her neighbour went into her house when her dog wouldn't stop barking and found her. Her throat had been cut."

"Oh my God." Charlotte thought for one horrifying moment that she was going to throw up all over Ren.

"Vince? Is Vince okay?" She clutched the front of his shirt.

"Yes. He's at the station. They're bringing Mel and the kids to him right now, and then they'll take them to a safe house."

"Thank God." She leaned against him.

"But Darlene -"

Fresh new terror made her body tense. "Is she dead?"

"No. But she and her boyfriend were run off the road. Their car went over an embankment, and they were seriously injured. Both of them are in surgery right now."

"What about Rita?"

"I don't know. I was out on patrol with one of the beat cops, and I didn't know what was going on until I got back to the station. They were just realizing the pattern when I arrived. I didn't wait. I just left for your house."

He hugged her again. "Thank God I didn't wait."

He led her down the hallway. "You need to gather some clothes, and we have to get out of here right now."

"But – but you killed the guy. I'm safe now, aren't I?"

"I don't know, honey. Steve obviously has hired multiple people – there could be more waiting to finish the job if the first guy fails."

"This can't be happening," she said as Ren looked into her room before tugging her into it. "Steve's in prison. How is he even doing this to us?"

"He's got a lot of pull, even on the inside. He's been in prison multiple times and knows how to work the system." Ren checked out her bedroom window before closing the curtains and turning on the light.

He opened the closet and searched it briefly before finding a duffle bag. "Here, use this to put some clothes and toiletries in."

"Are we going to the police station?" She stuffed clothes into the bag as Ren checked the window again.

"No. I'm taking you somewhere safe."

"What about the – the man on the porch? We can't just leave him there," she said.

"I'll call it in as soon as you're safe." He glanced at her. "Hurry, Charlotte."

* * *

Charlotte watched with apprehension as Ren clipped her duffle bag to the back of his motorcycle. She didn't resist when he slipped the plain black helmet on her head and buckled it before slipping on his own.

He straddled the bike and motioned for her to join him. "Come on, honey. We need to go." He glanced at the sky. "We need to beat the storm."

"Can't we take my car?" she said.

He shook his head. "No, honey."

"I've never been on a motorcycle before," she said.

"It's perfectly safe. Climb on behind me."

She continued to hesitate, and he reached out and snagged her hand. "I promise you it'll be okay."

She took a deep breath and swung her leg over the seat. She sat down gingerly and put her arms around Ren's waist, clasping them against his flat abdomen.

"Feet up on the pegs," he said.

She did as he asked and then jumped when the motorcycle roared to life. She slipped a little closer, her grip tightening around him, and he gently squeezed her clasped hands before shouting, "Okay, honey?"

"Yes," she shouted back.

He released the kickstand, and the bike rocked beneath their weight. He drove down the street, and Charlotte looked back at her house. She had a bad feeling she would never see it again.

* * *

CHARLOTTE LOOKED AROUND HER SURROUNDINGS WITH NUMB curiosity. Ren had driven for nearly three hours, guiding his motorcycle out of the city and beyond the surrounding suburbs. She had no clue where they were. Once they were out of the suburbs, she rested her cheek on Ren's back and closed her eyes. She decided that if she hadn't just nearly died and then watched Ren kill a man with his bare hands, she would have enjoyed the ride.

Instead, she'd felt that familiar numbness stealing over her. It was the same numbness she experienced after Rick's death, and although she knew it wasn't healthy, she'd embraced it and cocooned herself in its warmth.

Twenty minutes ago, Ren turned off the main road onto a narrow, bumpy dirt road. They drove deep into the woods, the road growing progressively narrower, and she had begun to think he would be making her camp in a tent among the trees when the road stopped abruptly in front of the cabin. She climbed stiffly off the back of Ren's motorcycle, tugged off her helmet and stared at the small cabin in front of them.

A loud clap of thunder split the sky, making her jump and cry out. With stunning ferocity, the sky opened, and a torrent of cold rain descended on them. Ren unbuckled her duffle bag, grabbed her hand, and they ran through the rain to the cabin. Despite their quickness, the rain was like a heavy sheet, and they were soaking wet when they reached the front door. Ren ran his fingers along the top of the doorframe and snagged a small silver key. He unlocked the front door and ushered Charlotte in.

She stood shivering in the hallway, her breath pluming like smoke in the chilly air of the cabin. It was hard to believe that it was almost the middle of summer. The storm seemed to have sucked all the warmth from the air, and she was glad when Ren shut and locked the door, muffling the sound of the rain.

"You own this place?" she said.

He nodded. "Yes. Well, my grandparents owned it, but I inherited it when they died."

He led her into the small living room and pointed to the couch against the far wall. "Sit on the couch while I make a fire."

"I'll ruin the upholstery," she said.

He kissed a drop of water from the tip of her nose. "It's only water, honey."

He pushed her gently down on the couch, and she watched as he lit a fire in the fireplace. She wondered where he had learned to do that and then decided she didn't care. The cold rain had shocked the numbness from her system, but it was slowly creeping back in. As Ren carefully coaxed the fire into life, she lay on the couch and curled into a ball on her side. She was cold and oddly sleepy.

\* \* \*

HIS STOMACH IN KNOTS, REN ADDED ANOTHER LOG TO THE fire. He straightened and turned to face Charlotte, the knots tightening in his belly. Charlotte was curled into a small ball on the couch, her eyes closed and her face pale. She was shivering violently despite how quickly the fire was banishing the chill from the room.

He knelt beside her and shook her lightly. "Charlotte?"

She cracked one eye open. "Yeah?"

"Sit up, honey."

She sat up obediently, and he cupped her face as she stared at him. A shiver snaked down his back. She had a look in her eyes, a terrible blankness that was horribly familiar to him, and his hands tightened on her arms. It was the same look she had worn when Steve pointed the gun at her head. Fear skimmed down his body.

"Charlotte!" he said sharply.

"What?" Her voice was flat and dull.

"You need to get out of your wet clothes. You're freezing." He rubbed her arms roughly through her wet jacket.

"I'm tired," she said.

"I know. You can have a hot shower, a bite to eat, and then go to bed." He helped her stand and led her to the bathroom.

"You have running water here?" Her lips were blue, and she shook violently as she toed off her shoes and shrugged out of her jacket.

"Yeah. Running water, electricity, and a pretty good internet connection, considering how far out we are. All the comforts of home."

"Are you calling Vince?" She examined the shower and tub enclosure.

"Yes. I'll call the station right now. I'll let them know you're safe and tell them about the man who tried to kill you."

"Yeah, sure, okay." She turned the shower on and tested the water with her hand, her movements listless and turtle slow.

"Charlotte? Honey, are you all right?"

"Why wouldn't I be? Sure, I almost died, and I watched you kill a man, but that's like a typical Thursday night for me." She brayed loud laughter with more than a hint of hysteria.

"Charlotte -"

"Go, Ren. Call Vince - he'll be worried about the both of us." She turned away, and, the worry eating at him like acid, he stepped out of the bathroom and shut the door.

\* \* \*

CHARLOTTE STOOD UNDER THE HOT SPRAY OF WATER. SHE knew she should wash her hair and body, but she couldn't seem to make her limbs move. For the last ten minutes, she'd alternated between paralyzing swoops of fear and barely suppressed hysterical laughter.

The shower curtain drew back, and Ren stepped naked into the shower. He poured shampoo into his palm and washed her long blonde hair without speaking. She tipped her head back so he could rinse it clean before putting conditioner in it. He took the soap and ran it over her naked body. She supposed she should feel embarrassed, but the terror and hysteria were still very close to the surface, so she kept her eyes closed and concentrated on her breathing.

He rinsed the conditioner from her hair and then cupped her face. "Are you warmer, Charlotte?"

"Yes. Thank you," she said.

She looked down. Ren's cock was half-hard, and she reached out with a trembling hand and wrapped her fingers around it. It stiffened into a rock hard erection at her touch, and his breath hissed out between his teeth.

"I'm sorry, honey," he said. "I have a hard time controlling myself around you."

She looked up at him. His eyes were radiating warmth and love, and she smiled weakly. "It's fine. It makes me feel -"

To her horror, her voice cracked, and she burst into loud sobs. Ren wrapped his arms around her and rocked her gently as water sprayed over them.

"I'm sorry, I'm so sorry," she sobbed against his throat as she clung to his naked, wet body.

"It's all right," he said. "Let it out."

She cried for nearly five minutes, ugly and loud bawling that tore from her throat and wracked her body with shudders. When her sobbing finally slowed, she turned and ducked her head under the now lukewarm water to rinse her face.

She turned back to Ren, staring at his chest in embarrassment until he put a gentle finger under her chin and raised her head. "Better?"

She nodded. Oddly enough, she did feel better. The numbness was still there, she could feel it creeping back in, but the horrible bouts of terror and hysteria had disappeared.

He shut off the water and pulled back the shower curtain. He had brought her duffel bag into the bathroom, and he stepped out of the tub, quickly drying his body before helping her out of the tub and wrapping her in her towel. She dried herself off as he used a smaller towel to squeeze the water out of her hair.

She dug through her duffel bag, pulled out the thin cotton nightgown she had grabbed and slipped it over her head. She reached for her comb, and Ren tugged it from her hands and combed her thick hair before squeezing out the excess water. He took her hand and led her out of the bathroom. A loud bang of thunder made her jump, and he pressed a kiss against her forehead.

"Are you hungry, Charlotte? There isn't much in the way of food, but I could heat a can of soup."

Her stomach rolled with nausea at the thought of food. "No. Not at all."

He frowned a little but let it go. "Okay. I'll show you to your bedroom."

Still naked, he led her down the hallway and pushed open the first door on the left. It was obviously his bedroom. The colour scheme was all male – dark blues and greys with no hint of a woman's touch. There was a fireplace in this room as well, and Ren must have started a fire in it before he joined her in the shower because it was crackling loudly, and the room was deliciously warm. Directly across the room from the fireplace was the bed. It was a large, ancient bed with a plain oak headboard and matching footboard.

"Is this your room?" she said.

"Yes. This one will be warmer for you. I'll stay in the guest room," he said.

She looked up at him, her lips trembling. "I don't want you to leave me."

"Then I won't," he said. They crossed the room together, and he shifted back the quilt and the sheet so she could climb in. She scooted over, and he climbed in after her. He laid on his back, and she curled up into him, throwing one thigh over his and one arm around his waist before burrowing her face in the curve of his neck.

The sheets were cool, but Ren was warm, and the bed was delightfully comfortable. She sank into its softness and pressed her body closer to Ren. "Promise me you'll stay."

"I promise I'll never leave you, Charlotte."

# CHAPTER 11

Charlotte woke abruptly, unsure of what woke her up. She was still pressed against Ren, his arm around her and his hand resting against her hip, and she peered at him in the dim light. His chest rose in slow and even breaths, and sleep had made his face younger.

She had no idea what time it was, but the fire was low in the fireplace, and she felt more like herself. Rain still beat against the window. She could hear it even through the shutters, but lying in Ren's bed with his heart beating solidly against her palm made her feel safe despite the horrors of the night.

She studied his face in the flickering light from the fire. She stared at his chin scar and the one running under his jaw and wondered how he had gotten them. She reached up and traced first the one on his jaw and then the one on his chin. He opened his eyes and smiled at her.

"Hi."

"Hi. I'm sorry. I didn't mean to wake you."

"I'm a light sleeper. Hazard of the job," he said.

"How did you get these?" She retraced the scar on his chin.

"Fell out of a tree when I was eleven."

"Did you need stitches?"

"Yes. Four on my chin and seven on my jaw."

She lifted her head and kissed the scar on his jaw. His hand tightened briefly on her hip. Moving her lips to his mouth seemed natural, so she did. She kissed his firm lips, a slow beat of desire rippling through her when he kissed her back for a brief moment.

He pulled back. "Charlotte – stop, honey."

"Don't you want me?"

"You know I do. But, I'm not sure this is the best time to -"

"It is." She kissed him again, her tongue licking at his mouth. "Please, Ren."

With a quiet groan, he rolled her onto her back and braced his big body over hers.

He began to kiss her, slow and soft brushes of his mouth against hers until the heat coursed through her body. She kneaded his shoulders with her hands and opened her mouth wide, silently urging him to kiss her deeper and harder.

When he finally slipped his tongue into her mouth, her hips arched against him, and she moaned encouragingly. He continued to kiss her, not letting his hands touch her and keeping himself perfectly still while she thrust her hips against him. Her core was soaking wet, her thighs damp with her need, and her want, and she couldn't understand why he wasn't touching her in the way she so obviously wanted.

"Ren, please," she said.

"Charlotte, I think this might be a bad idea. I feel like I'm taking advantage of you, and I -"

She muttered a curse under her breath and pushed at his chest. "Get off me, Ren."

He rolled off her and onto his back, his eyes dark with worry and regret. "Honey, I want to make love to you. But it's -"

She pushed the covers back, stared hungrily at his erect cock, and straddled him before he could sit up. Her wet pussy rubbed against his cock, and he groaned, his hips rising before he could stop them.

She grinned with satisfaction, grabbed his cock, and impaled herself on it. He cried out, his hands closing in tight fists around the bed sheets as she braced her hands on his chest and pushed herself down until she was filled completely. She yanked her shirt over her head, and he stared greedily at her small, pert breasts as she took his hands and placed them on her breasts. He immediately rubbed her nipples, his nostrils flaring when she threw her head back and arched her back. He pulled and pinched them lightly until she leaned over and guided one breast to his mouth. He sucked her nipple into his mouth, rubbing his tongue across it with a roughness that had her toes curling. She pulled away, the pleasure of his warm, sweet mouth suddenly too much.

She stared down at him as he steadied her with his hands on her hips before rocking his pelvis against her. Her hands traced his tattoos and the small scar on his chest before she pinched his flat nipple. He jerked against her, and she gasped as his hard cock thickened within her.

"You feel so good inside of me, Ren," she whispered as she rose up and down his thick shaft in a slow, rippling motion. She braced her hands on his chest and rode him hard, her head thrown back and her small breasts thrust outwards. Her nipples were taut and begging for his touch, and he reached up and tugged on them lightly.

Her pussy fluttered enticingly, and then she stiffened, her core clamping down and rippling around him as she climaxed hard around his cock. His hands dug into her hips as she shook and shivered on top of him.

When she had collapsed weakly against him, he rolled her onto her back and nestled his large body between her thighs. She spread her legs wide and gave him a soft smile as her small hand reached between them and gripped his cock.

He groaned, and it brought another smile to her lips. She guided him to her wet entrance and pressed her small body upward. He eased in, his eyes closing as he moved with slow and gentle thrusts.

"Charlotte, wait. You should be on top again," he said.

She hooked her lean thighs around his hips and drew him deeper into her. "Why?"

"I don't want to hurt you," he groaned.

"I'm tougher than I look, Detective."

She squeezed her pussy around him, drawing a low moan from his throat. He pushed in deeply until his entire cock was sheathed, and she made a soft cooing noise of pleasure into his ear.

"That's right, Ren. Just like that," she said. "Make me feel good. Please, honey."

He moaned and plunged in and out of her. She arched her hips and tightened her thighs around him.

Charlotte braced her feet on the bed and gripped Ren's broad shoulders. He was moving faster and harder now, and his breathing was ragged as he propped himself above her.

She stared up at him and urged him on with soft cries and moans. She knew he was holding back, could feel it in the tense muscles of his shoulders and the way he didn't quite let himself sink fully into her, and she reached up and stroked his face with her fingertips.

"Don't hold back, honey," she whispered. "I won't break."

He groaned at her words and thrust hard into her as her body yielded beneath him. He reached between them, and his rough fingers found her clit. She cried out, her hips arching upwards as he stroked and rubbed the swollen, wet nub.

"Oh God, oh Ren, oh please," she moaned.

He kissed her hard on the mouth, his tongue seeking out hers as she tensed under him and then cried out into his mouth as her body stiffened and her pussy clamped down hard around him. The muscles of her pussy milked his hard length as she came, and he climaxed with a harsh groan.

He collapsed against her and buried his face into the curve of her shoulder. She wrapped her limbs around him as he kissed her fragrant skin repeatedly before finally rolling off of her. She curled up onto her side, grabbing his arm and pulling him into her until he was spooning her.

"Did I hurt you?" He pushed her hair back and kissed her temple.

"Of course not," she said. "I told you – I'm tougher than I look, Ren."

"I believe you." He cupped one small breast and buried his face into her back as she smiled and closed her eyes.

# CHAPTER 12

C harlotte eased the helmet off her head as Ren shut the
bike off and put the kickstand down. She swung off
the bike, and Ren removed his helmet and climbed off it
before unstrapping the duffel bag holding their groceries.

She took his hand, and he squeezed it gently as he led her
to the cabin. It had been over a week since he brought her to
the cabin, and holding his hand, touching him, had become
as natural to her as breathing.

He started to unpack the groceries in the kitchen, and she
could feel a smile crossing her lips. The back of her shoulder
was itching, and she felt a little sensitive as she shrugged off
her jacket, but she assumed that was normal.

Ren caught her smile and raised his eyebrows at her.
"What are you smiling about?"

"I can't believe I did that." She grinned at him, and he
laughed.

"Let's take a look at it." He helped her slip out of her t-
shirt and then turned her around before gently peeling away
the small bandage that covered her back.

"How does it look?"

"It looks beautiful. Come to the bathroom, and I'll show you."

He positioned her in front of the bathroom mirror and held up the smaller hand mirror. She peered into it at the reflection of her back in the mirror mounted on the wall.

The daisy tattoo was small, and the skin around it was red and swollen, but she grinned again at the sight of it. She had seen the tattoo shop the last time they had driven to the small town of Tamworth. Tamworth was just over an hour from Ren's cabin, and they had gone there for supplies the day after they arrived. Although she'd never been to Tamworth before, Ren had insisted she cover her blonde hair with an oversized scarf, and he had bought her a pair of sunglasses that nearly covered her entire face. Despite his concerns over being seen, it'd been remarkably easy to convince him to set up an appointment at the tattoo shop for her.

"What do you think?" he said.

"I love it. I really do."

"If you're not careful, you'll end up covered in them like me." He kissed her forehead.

"Yeah, I'm not that brave."

"You were great with this one. Even with your fear of needles," he said.

"I still don't think I'll get another one. At least not for a while." She reached for his t-shirt, and he lifted his arms so she could pull it over his head.

She leaned forward and kissed his skull tattoo before licking a slow path across his throat. He groaned, his hand cupping the back of her head as she nibbled at his neck.

Her hands reached for his belt, and she unbuckled it before unbuttoning and unzipping his jeans and shoving them down his thighs. She dropped to her knees, and he groaned harshly with need when her hands toyed with the band of his briefs.

"Charlotte," he moaned.

She smiled and tugged his underwear down, freeing his erect cock. She stroked the shaft with her fingertips and smiled again when his breath hissed out between his teeth. The tip of his erection was glistening, and she swiped her tongue across it lightly.

"Oh God," he muttered as his hips jerked and his hands dropped to her hair. He pulled the clip from her blonde strands and threaded his fingers through her hair as she slid her mouth down over him.

Charlotte used her tongue to lightly tease the head of his cock as she sucked. Above her, Ren's groans and how his hands tightened and loosened compulsively in her hair set her on fire with need. She sucked harder, sliding her lips back and forth over his velvet skin until Ren muttered a curse and pulled her to her feet.

He kissed her hard on the mouth, sliding his tongue in to duel with hers as his hands yanked down her jeans and panties. She kicked them off her feet, giggling when she accidentally kicked him in the shin, and he growled playfully at her before unclipping her bra.

He lifted her easily and sat her on the bathroom counter before stepping between her thighs. He kissed her again, his cock rubbing against her wetness as he cupped one breast and kneaded it lightly.

An image of the salon, of being in this exact position, flooded through her, and she stiffened against him.

"What?" he said.

"I – this just reminds me of the salon." She leaned her forehead against his broad chest as he rubbed her back.

"I'm sorry." He kissed the top of her head.

"It's all right." She pushed the mental image of Steve

saying he wanted his turn out of her head. "It's just – you know."

He nodded, and she gasped in surprise when he lifted her. She wrapped her legs around his waist as he carried her out of the bathroom and into the bedroom.

"I'm sorry, I should have thought of that." Guilt covered his features, and she traced the scar on his jaw.

"No, it's okay. Honestly, it's just – sometimes I don't like to be reminded of that day in any way," she said as he entered the bedroom.

"I don't either. You almost died that day, Charlotte."

"So did you. So did Vince," she said.

He stood beside the bed and kissed her lightly before placing her on her feet. "Maybe we shouldn't do this right now. Why don't we go back to the kitchen and -"

She put her hand over his mouth and scowled mockingly at him. "There's no way I'm stopping. There are plenty of other positions."

She poked him playfully, and a grin crossed his face. "That's true. Perhaps we should do lady's choice."

"I like that idea." She trailed her fingers down his broad chest. "I want you to take me on my hands and knees, Ren. What do you think?"

Desire flooded through him, and she flushed at the look on his face before kissing his chest. "I think you like that idea."

"Yes," he said hoarsely. "God, yes."

He turned her a bit roughly, and she didn't protest when he lifted her and dropped her to her hands and knees on the bed. She spread her thighs eagerly as he pushed up against her and stroked her ass with his warm hands.

He guided his cock into her warmth and her wetness, and she moaned and pushed back against him, sheathing him fully. He reached beneath her and cupped her breasts as he slid in and out of her. He kissed just below her new tattoo as she turned her head and stared at him.

"You're so beautiful, Charlotte," he said.

"Thank you. I... oh!"

His fingers had slid to her swollen clit and were rubbing the throbbing nub with firm pressure. She arched her back and squeezed her muscles around him as pleasure rushed through her.

"Ren," she moaned.

He thrust harder into her, and she reached back for his hand. He laced her fingers with his as they lost themselves in the pleasure of their union.

\* \* \*

"WHY DID YOU BECOME AN UNDERCOVER DETECTIVE?"

They were lying naked in the bed. Charlotte sprawled across his chest and propped herself up on her elbows, staring curiously at him.

He shrugged. "My parents were gone, and I wasn't in a relationship. I figured I was perfect for undercover work."

"Did you enjoy it?"

"Yes and no. I liked bringing down the criminals, but I hated associating with them and the things I had to do while I was with them."

"Why did you leave?"

"I had been in it long enough," he lied. He didn't think telling Charlotte he had left for her and only her was the most brilliant idea. "After seeing Vince shot and watching Steve threaten you and the others without being able to do anything about it – I'd had enough."

"But you did do something about it," she replied. "You shot Steve."

He gave her a faint smile. "I guess."

"Have you ever been in a serious relationship before?"

He shook his head. "Not since high school. And I'm not sure that high school love is considered serious. I dated a few different women, but once I went undercover, that ended what little social life I had."

"You never slept with anyone while you were undercover?" She wasn't exactly sure what being in a motorcycle club was like, but there were women galore if TV was any indication.

"No. The first few times I went undercover, it wasn't with a club. It was mostly trapping drug dealers, that sort of thing. Once I joined Steve's club, he had plenty of women who were willing, but I didn't sleep with any of them."

"Why not? It seemed like that made Steve suspicious," she said.

"It did, but I was never really into the one-night stand thing," Ren said. "I like to get to know a woman first before I sleep with her."

"I guess I'm the exception to that, huh?" Charlotte said.

Ren stroked her hair. "I wanted you from the moment I saw you, Charlotte. But I hate what Steve made us do that day in the salon. I hate that you were forced to be with me to save Vince's life, and if I could go back and change it, I would. I should have killed Steve instead of going along with his sick little game. I wish every day that I had. As much as I wanted you - wanted to be with you - I regret what happened between us in the salon."

"I don't."

He jerked against her. "What do you mean?"

"I don't regret it," she said. "I know that makes me sound like I'm the biggest slut in town, but -"

"You're not," he said. "Don't say that, Charlotte."

"Before that day, I was just... existing, you know? Rick had been dead for three months, and I was numb. I hadn't felt anything since the day he died, and then you touched me, and I finally felt something other than that horrible numbness."

Tears started to slide down her cheeks, and she wiped them away almost angrily. "I didn't want to die. I didn't," she frowned at him as if he had argued with her, "but I didn't care if I did. Does that make sense?"

"Yes. I think so. How did Rick die?"

"Bone cancer. It started in his leg, and they did chemo and radiation, and finally, in desperation, they took his leg above the knee. That was hard for Rick. He was active, played lots of sports and was in a running club, but I told him it didn't matter. I told him that he would learn to use a prosthetic and be back doing what he loved in no time. All that mattered was that he survived."

Ren reached out and wiped away the tears that were falling freely now from her eyes. "Only he didn't survive. Three months after they took his leg, they found cancer in his lungs and his brain. Six months after that, he was dead."

"I'm sorry," Ren said.

"Thank you," she said. "After he died, my therapist said I had to expect lots of different emotions while I worked through my grief, only there wasn't any. I just went through each day wondering when I would start to be angry or sad or lonely, and it never happened. It was awful."

She took a deep breath and smiled faintly at him. "After I woke up in the hospital after I found out that you were dead, I waited for the numbness to come back. I figured it would, you know? But it didn't. Maybe it was the almost dying or watching Vince almost die - I'm not sure - but all those emotions came flooding back in, and I grieved. I grieved for Rick, and I grieved for you."

She rested her face on his chest, and he rubbed her back. "I'm so sorry."

"Enough with the apologies, Ren. I need a spreadsheet to keep track of your unnecessary apologies," she said.

He laughed a little, and she wiped away the tears before lifting her head and smiling at him. "I just wanted you to know why I don't regret what happened between us that day. I know that day was awful and horrible in so many ways, but the part between you and me in that back room? I needed that."

He didn't reply, and she flushed. "Don't worry. I'm seeing a therapist about my weirdness."

"I don't think you're weird."

"You just don't know me well enough." She stuck her tongue out at him and rested her head against his chest, trailing her fingers through the dark hair.

He stared at the ceiling. He hadn't realized, until now, how deeply his guilt ran over what had happened at the salon that day. Knowing that Charlotte didn't regret it filled him with relief so strong he felt nearly giddy, and he inadvertently hugged her closer.

"You okay?" she said.

"Yes. Are you?"

"I'm getting there," she said.

* * *

"WHAT?" REN HELD HIS CELL PHONE CLOSER TO HIS EAR AND peered out the kitchen window. Charlotte was hanging their clothes on the clothesline, and she gave him a brief wave. He waved back, forcing himself to smile at her as he turned away.

"Steve is dead." Vince, his voice cutting in and out, repeated.

"How?"

"They're not sure. They think it was one of the other

inmates, but they don't know who or why yet," Vince said. "It happened two days ago."

"Jesus. Well, that's good – I guess," Ren said.

"It is. They're letting Mel, the kids, and I leave the safe house. Rita's already returned home, and they're no longer keeping guards posted outside of Darlene and her boyfriend's hospital rooms."

"How is Darlene?" Ren asked. "Charlotte's pretty anxious about her."

"She's good," Vince said. "She's recovering nicely, and they think she and her boyfriend will leave the hospital by the end of the week."

"Charlotte will be happy to hear that." Ren glanced out the window again. Charlotte was hanging up the last of the clothes, and he could feel his stomach drop at the thought of taking her back home. They had spent nearly two weeks together, but she hadn't made any declarations of love, and he had no idea how she felt about him. He wanted more time with her. After ten months of missing her, of dreaming about her, the last two weeks were a dream come true.

"Ren?"

He forced himself to concentrate on Vince. "Yeah?"

"I asked if you're going to bring Charlotte back tomorrow."

"Uh... the thing is, how do we know that the men Steve hired aren't going to try to finish the job? Even with him dead?"

"Chuck and Robbie are confident that it won't happen. The men Steve hired aren't exactly loyal."

Chuck and Robbie were the two detectives assigned to the case, and Ren didn't know a thing about them. "And you trust these guys? They know what they're doing?"

"Yes. They've got good connections on the street, Ren. I

promise you. They're thorough, and they figured out who the other two men were that Steve hired and -"

"But they couldn't find them?" Ren said.

"They tried," Vince said. "One of them left town the day that Steve died, and the other – he was killed in an altercation with the police last night. He was robbing a convenience store, and there was an off-duty cop there. They wouldn't be sending us back home if they thought there was a chance that there was still a threat, all right?"

"Yeah. The thing is, I don't think Charlotte is ready to come back home. She's still fragile, and I don't believe she ever really worked through what happened that day at the salon."

The silence over the phone stretched out until he was sure he had lost the connection. "Vince?"

"Yeah, I'm here. I think you're wrong, Ren. I think Charlotte has done remarkably well with everything that's happened."

"I still don't -"

"But I do think she needs a vacation," Vince said. "I think being away from everything that has happened the last year is good for her, and I think you're good for her. Tell her what's happened, but ask her to give it another week or so before she comes home. Tell her that Vince said this is the vacation he suggested."

Vince's voice had a hint of laughter, and Ren nodded. "I'll try. Charlotte is, well, she's stubborn."

Vince laughed. "You're telling me. Take care, Ren. Text me if you convince Charlotte to stay, and I'll tell them at the salon."

"Will do. Thanks, Vince." Ren hung up the phone as Charlotte entered the cabin, her cheeks rosy and the scent of fresh air clinging to her.

"Who was that?" She set the wicker laundry basket on the floor.

"Vince."

"How is he? How are Mel and the kids? Is everyone okay? Is there news about Darlene?" She chewed at her bottom lip.

"Everyone's fine. Darlene is doing much better. They think she and her boyfriend will be released from the hospital soon." He folded her into his embrace and kissed her forehead. "There's been some news about Steve."

"What is it?" She leaned her head against his chest.

"They've figured out who the two remaining guys that Steve hired are. Once they – they find them, we'll probably be able to return home."

"Holy shit. Seriously? But what if Steve hires more men? What then?" Charlotte said.

He made himself smile at her. "They'll take measures in prison to ensure that doesn't happen."

"Are you sure?"

"Yes." It wasn't true. Prisoners like Steve, men who had spent most of their lives in and out of various prisons, had an almost eerie way of getting what they wanted – locked up or not. Of course, Steve was dead, and Ren was lying to the woman he loved.

Her smile faltered. "What's wrong?" She reached up and felt his forehead. "Are you sick? You're pale?"

He shook his head. "I'm fine. Just a little tired, maybe."

"Come lie down with me." She squeezed his hand. "We'll have a nap, and then we'll have grilled steaks and wine for dinner. I feel like celebrating."

She smiled happily at him, and a wave of nausea went through him. He pushed it down and tried to give her a natural smile. "I like that idea. Just give me a minute, okay? I'll meet you in the bedroom."

She studied him carefully for a moment before nodding. She walked down the hallway, exaggeratedly rolling her hips as she pulled off her t-shirt and dropped it onto the floor. She was braless under it, and he smiled a little at the sight of her tattoo.

She wiggled her ass at him. "Don't be too long, handsome. I have a great idea to help you fall asleep."

He smiled again as she disappeared into the bedroom. The smile fell from his face, and he stared at his phone. His fingers trembling, he sent a quick text to Vince before shutting off the phone and tossing it on the coffee table.

He was doing the right thing. He hated lying to Charlotte, but she needed more time. Another week at the cabin would do her good.

*Her or you? Tell yourself the truth, Ren. You're lying to Charlotte, the woman you love, because you want more time with her. You want to make her fall in love with you, and you think that if she goes back to her old life, back to her friends and her job, you won't have a chance with her. You're playing a dangerous game. Sooner or later, she's going to find out you lied and –*

He shut his inner voice down with a snap and took a deep breath before heading toward the bedroom. He was doing this for Charlotte. She needed more time.

# CHAPTER 13

"Are you sure you're okay, Ren?" Charlotte toyed with the stem of her wineglass and gave him a worried look. He had been quiet and almost withdrawn over dinner, and as she sat down on the couch next to him, she rubbed his large thigh.

"I'm good." He put his arm around her, and she leaned into his embrace. "How are you?"

"I'm happy," she said. She rubbed his thigh again and glanced around the cabin. "I'm glad you brought me here, Ren. This place is, well, it's special."

He didn't reply, and she squeezed his leg. "Did you come here often as a child?"

"I did. I spent a lot of time with my grandparents growing up. My dad was a cop and worked long hours, and my mom was a nurse and did a lot of shift work."

"Do you have any other family?"

He shook his head. "Not here. It's partly why I'm so close to Vince and Mel. I have an aunt on my mom's side, but she's lived in Europe most of my life. How about you? Are you close to your parents?"

"My mom died when I was four. She had a brain aneurysm, and it killed her instantly. My dad remarried when I was eight. Cathy is nice enough, but we never really connected. She and my dad moved to Florida ten years ago to be closer to her family. Dad and I kept in touch pretty well the first few years, but then we drifted apart. He came down for Rick's funeral, and we promised that we'd be better at keeping in touch, and for a while, we were. I even went to Florida and stayed with him and Cathy for a few days. But I think too much time has passed, and we no longer have much in common. He calls about once a month, but it's pretty awkward."

"What about Rick's parents?"

Charlotte smiled a little. "They didn't care much for me."

"What? Why?" Ren said.

"Rick was an only child and very close to his mom. She saw me as competition, I think."

"Gross," Ren said.

Charlotte laughed. "Yeah, it was kind of gross when you think about it. Rick was pretty good about trying to keep the peace between us. He was easy-going and did his best to keep his mom happy while not allowing her to invade our space or push between us."

She stared at the fireplace. "I know it was hard on him, though. He loved his mom very much, and it was stressful for him to see her upset."

"How long were you and Rick married for?"

"Six years."

"Did you want kids?" he said.

"Yes," she said. "Rick and I loved kids, and we planned to have at least three. We were trying to get pregnant when we found out about the cancer. We put the plan for kids on hold until after he recovered."

She leaned a little closer to him. "Mel asked me once,

about six months after Ren died, if I wished that we had gone ahead and tried to have a baby. As terrible as this sounds, I'm glad we didn't. Rick was horribly sick for two years, and I couldn't imagine how difficult it would have been to be caring for a baby as well."

"That doesn't make you sound terrible."

"Doesn't it? Rick's mom thought it did. She took me aside one day after it became clear that Rick would die and told me that I should be trying to get pregnant. She wanted a grand-child. She wanted someone to remind her of her son, and I understood that. Part of me wanted it as well, but even then, she was fooling herself about how sick her son was. It was too late, you know? He didn't have the energy to eat. Hell, he couldn't go to the bathroom on his own. There was no way we could try for a baby."

"I can't imagine how difficult it was for you," he said.

"Rick's mom helped a lot, and we had nurses who came in at the end and helped care for him. He wanted to die at home, and I made damn sure that I did whatever it took to make that happen."

"You must miss him." He stroked her arm.

"I do." She stared at her bare ring finger. "But after he died, the overwhelming feeling was one of relief. He had been so sick, and I couldn't help feeling relieved that he wasn't suffering anymore. My therapist said that was a common reaction. Like I told you before, the missing him and the true grieving didn't come until about five months later."

They were silent for a few minutes, and she stared up at him when he shifted away from her.

"What's wrong?"

"After the salon thing, I spent months thinking about you. Thinking about seeing you again – about touching you and being with you – while you mourned your dead husband. I'm feeling pretty awful about that right now."

She shook her head. "I don't think you should. We obviously had a connection at the salon. I think it's a normal reaction after what happened between us. Besides, the day after I found out you were alive, I was having my own fantasies."

"Really?"

"Yes, really." She leaned back against him before giving him a curious little side glance. "So, what were your fantasies about?"

After their afternoon lovemaking, she hadn't bothered to get dressed, just snagged his t-shirt while he had tugged on shorts. He stroked her bare thigh. "The usual. Me taking you every which way from Sunday and you screaming about what a stud I was during your multiple orgasms."

She laughed, and he grinned at her as she straddled his lap. "Stud, huh?"

"I'm also willing to accept stallion, sex machine, or master of the clit."

She laughed again before lightly tracing his tattoos. "You are nothing like you seem, Ren."

"What do you mean?"

"What do I mean?" She arched her eyebrow at him. "You're huge, muscular, and covered in tattoos. Don't you think that projects a certain image?"

He shrugged. "I suppose."

She rolled her eyes. "You know that it does. People think you're a badass motherfucker. Pardon my language." She giggled to herself. "If people only knew the real you."

He gave her a mock scowl and tugged lightly on her blonde tresses. "Hey, I am a badass motherfucker."

She snorted. "Is that what you tell yourself when you're

rescuing kittens from trees and helping little old ladies cross the street?"

He grinned at her, and she leaned forward and kissed him. "Face it, Ren. You're a soft-hearted, big old teddy bear."

"Only around you." He slipped his hands under her shirt to rub the tops of her warm thighs.

That, she decided, was probably closer to the truth. Ren was undoubtedly kind, and he treated her like she was a fragile doll he needed to protect, but he had also killed a man on her front porch. He just broke his neck like it was nothing. A shudder went down her back, and Ren squeezed her legs.

"Are you all right?"

"Yes." Despite what she had seen Ren do, she had no fear of him. In fact, she had never felt safer in her life. Ren loved her and would do whatever was needed to keep her safe.

He loved her.

She mulled that over in her head. Ren really did love her despite only knowing her briefly, and that knowledge frightened and excited her. She didn't know if she loved him or not. She was very fond of him, and she was undoubtedly addicted to his skills in the bedroom, but love could be easily confused with lust.

*You're very fond of him? The man saved your life twice, he quite obviously adores and loves you, and all you can say is you're fond of him?*

Her inner voice made a snort of disgust. Her therapist would tell her that she was pushing down her real feelings and thoughts on the matter out of guilt. Guilt over wanting someone after Rick, guilt over enjoying another man's touch. It wasn't fair to Ren, and she needed to figure out how the hell she felt about him before she hurt him badly.

"Charlotte?"

Ren stared worriedly at her, and she gave him what she

hoped was a seductive smile. They were stuck at this cabin for God knew how long, and despite how selfish it made her, she wanted to think about nothing but how good Ren made her feel.

"So, about these fantasies. Did any of them ever involve me naked in your lap in a secluded little cabin while you fucked me senseless?"

She tugged his t-shirt over her head and dropped it to the floor, smiling at the hungry look on his face as his gaze dropped to her breasts.

"Well, did they?" she said as she cupped her breasts.

"Yes." He tugged her hands away and cupped her breasts himself, pulling lightly on her nipples until they were hard and throbbing.

"Quite the imagination you have, Detective," she said. She could feel his erection against her, and she rubbed herself against his lap. He arched his hips into her, and she helped him ease his shorts down his legs. She stroked his cock, rubbing it firmly as she stared at him, and he made a quiet groan before urging her forward.

She slid his cock deep inside her warmth, her hands clutching at Ren's shoulders as she stretched around him. He kissed her throat, nibbling lightly, before pressing soft kisses against her mouth. She returned his kisses as they rocked against each other in a slow, deep rhythm. He cupped the back of her neck, and she couldn't look away from his warm gaze as they continued to move in the same slow rhythm.

His hand slipped between their bodies, and he touched her clit lightly. She moaned, her eyes falling shut as he touched her until she was tightening around him. He groaned, and she opened her eyes and smiled at him.

"I'm so close, Ren."

"Me too," he moaned. "Charlotte, I lo -"

He stopped, his face twisting, before he buried his face in her neck and pumped his hips against her.

"What?" She tugged on his hair until he raised his head.

"Nothing." He rubbed her swollen clit.

She moaned as the familiar tingling began deep in her pelvis. She was very close now, and she bit her lip and rocked her hips against him frantically.

"Say it, Ren," she gasped out. "Say it."

"I love you," he whispered.

He groaned with pleasure as her pussy tightened around him, and she made a loud, gasping cry as she came. He thrust into her, his entire body shaking, and wrapped his arms around her small body.

"I love you," he repeated before his back arched, and warm wetness filled her.

She collapsed against him, panting loudly, and he stroked her warm back

"Ren?" Charlotte said.

"Yeah?"

"You are such a stud."

* * *

"REN, I FEEL RIDICULOUS," CHARLOTTE SAID.

With his large arm around her slender neck, Ren said, "You need to learn this, Charlotte. Every woman should know some self-defence moves."

"You outweigh me by like seventy pounds," she said.

"It doesn't matter. If you hit a person in the right spots, it doesn't matter how much bigger they are than you," he said. "Let's try it again."

He drew her back against him until her back was tucked firmly against his chest. "If an attacker has you in a hold like this, where is he most vulnerable?"

"Here." She raised her foot and pretended to stomp on the top of his foot.

"Good. My arm loosens," he released his gentle hold around her neck, "and you do what?"

She elbowed him lightly in the midsection.

"Good. Make sure you put your weight into it, Charlotte. You want me to lose my breath, right?"

She nodded. "Yes."

"What else?"

"I can also go for the groin." She reached back with her hand and cupped his penis, giving it a light squeeze. "Of course, I'll use more of a punching motion."

She grinned up at him as she continued to stroke his cock. "But I like your penis so…"

He laughed and kissed her forehead. "My penis really likes you."

"I've noticed," she said tartly. He was hardening under her touch, and she gave him another firm squeeze. "Why don't we take a break, and your penis and I can show each other exactly how much we like one another."

He grinned and shook his head. "Nope. We need to keep practicing."

She pouted at him, and he laughed again. "Pouting will not get you out of this."

She shrugged as he turned her to face him. "Well, it didn't hurt to try."

He kissed the tip of her nose and pulled her flush against him. "If an attacker is holding you like this, what will you do?"

"If my hands are free, I'll use the heel of my hand to strike the nose."

She brought her hand up to his face, and he nodded before taking her hand and straightening her fingers a little more.

128

"Don't make so much of a fist. Keep your fingers curled just a little, and make sure you hit him with only the heel of your hand. Okay?"

"Okay."

"And if your arms are pinned down?" He put his arms around hers, pinning them to her sides, and she stared at him.

"I use my head to strike the nose."

"That's right. But make sure you -"

"Use the top of my head and not my forehead," she finished.

"Good." He smiled at her. "If you're lucky, it'll knock the assailant out. But even if it doesn't, it'll make him let go and his eyes water, giving you some time to run."

"But not before I punch him in the groin," she said.

He nodded. "It's the most effective way of dropping a male attacker to his knees."

She wriggled against him, and he loosened his grip so she could wrap her arms around his waist. He kissed her forehead. "We'll practice these moves every day, okay?"

"Sure." She squeezed his ass. "There are some other moves I was thinking we could practice, too."

He nodded. "Okay, but I wanted to talk to you about one more thing."

She stilled at his serious tone. "What is it?"

"I think you should learn how to use a gun," he said.

She gave him an uneasy look. "I – I don't know, Ren."

"I think it's a good idea, honey," he said. "You can take lessons, learn how to use it properly, and have a better chance of protecting yourself."

"Can I think about it?"

"Yes." He touched her face gently. "I know the thought of firing a gun can be unnerving, but you need to learn. I'd feel a lot better about leaving you alone at your house if you had a gun and knew how to use it properly."

She rested her forehead against his chest. "I hate this, Ren."

"I know. I'm sorry."

"It's not your fault." She hugged him before taking his hand. "C'mon, stud, there's something in the bedroom I want to show you."

He grinned at her. "What a coincidence – I've got something to show you as well."

"I just bet you do, my little stallion," she said.

"Little?" He growled, and she laughed when he hoisted her over his shoulder and slapped her ass. "I'll have you know my penis is slightly above average, woman."

She snickered. "Ooh, slightly above average, you say? How can I resist?"

He slapped her ass again and carried her toward the bedroom.

# CHAPTER 14

C harlotte wiped down the counter and draped the cloth over the sink. She stared out the window at Ren as there was a soft buzzing noise behind her. His cell phone was on the table, and she hesitated before walking over to it. Vince's name was on the screen, and with a slight frown, she hit the answer button.

"Vince? What's wrong?"

"Charlotte! Honey, it's so good to hear your voice," Vince said.

"It's good to hear yours too, but what's wrong?"

"Nothing's wrong. I was calling to check in."

Charlotte breathed a sigh of relief. "It's good. No problems here. How are Darlene and Mark? Ren said they were getting out of the hospital."

"They did. I haven't heard anything new, so I'm assuming they're both fine," Vince said.

"How are Mel and the kids?" Charlotte said.

"Oh good, good. Jade's leaving next week to go back to university and -"

"What?" Charlotte said.

"I said, Jade's leaving next week to return to university. It's early, but she's thinking of -"

"Are you sure that's a good idea?" Charlotte said. "What if someone Steve hired tries to hurt her to get back at you? Is she even allowed to leave the safe house?"

There was a long silence, and she checked the screen before holding the phone to her ear again. "Vince? Are you still there?"

"Yes. Charlotte, didn't Ren tell you?"

"Tell me what?"

"When I called last week, it was to tell him that Steve was dead."

"What?" Charlotte gripped the phone as her knees began to shake. She staggered to the window and stared out at Ren. He was still working on his bike, and she stared grimly at him before turning away.

"Steve's dead. Didn't Ren tell you?" Vince sad.

"No," she said. "No, he didn't."

"Another inmate killed Steve. We left the safe house last week, and Rita and Darlene are also in their own homes."

"What about the men he hired?" Charlotte said.

"They tracked down the last two men he hired. One of them left town the day Steve was murdered, and the other was killed in a robbery by an undercover cop," Vince said. "Charlotte, you really didn't know? Ren said he was going to tell you."

"He didn't." She couldn't hide the bitterness in her voice, and Vince cleared his throat.

"I thought you were just staying with Ren at the cabin because you needed more time to get over what had happened."

"No," she said. "Ren lied to me."

"Charlotte, I'm sure he had a good reason to -"

"Vince, I have to go," Charlotte said. "I'm coming home today, and I'll call you and Mel tomorrow, okay?"

"Charlotte, wait! Just talk to Ren, all right? I know he had a good reason for -"

"I'll call you later." Charlotte ended the call as Ren walked through the door. He stared at the phone in her hand.

"Who were you talking to?"

"Vince," she said.

He stiffened, his face losing some of its colour. "Charlotte -"

"You lied to me," she said.

"I'm sorry. I should have told you about Steve and that it was safe to go back home, but I was worried about you. I thought you needed more time to process what had happened, and I -"

"Don't." She held her hands up and backed away when he moved toward her. "Don't make this worse by lying again."

"I'm not," he said.

"You are." Her voice was rising, and she took a deep breath and wrapped her arms around her torso. "You kept me here like a prisoner because it's what you wanted. You think you're in love with me and thought if you kept me here long enough, I'd fall in love with you."

"I *am* in love with you," he said. "I wanted to keep you safe, honey."

"So, you lied to me?" she said. "You don't lie to the person you love, Ren."

"I'm sorry. I shouldn't have -"

"You're sorry! You're always sorry!" she shouted. "You had no right to keep this from me, Ren! Do you get that? Do you realize how badly you've fucked up?"

"I do, and I promise if you just give me a chance to make it right, I'll -"

"No. I trusted you, and you lied to me. I have a life, Ren. I have a life that maybe you don't think is great or you think would be better with you in it, but that's my decision to make. Mine – not yours."

He started to talk, and she glared at him. "Don't. Don't say another word. I'm packing my stuff and want you to take me home. Right now. I don't – I can't be around you anymore."

She stalked out of the kitchen and into the bedroom, slamming the door behind her.

* * *

"Charlotte, wait!" Ren yanked off his helmet as Charlotte dropped hers on the back of the seat and hurried up the walk of her house. He ran after her and touched her arm, wincing when she yanked it away.

"Please, I'm so sorry," he said. "Can I call you tomorrow and -"

"No." She dug her keys out of her purse. "Don't call me, Ren."

She found her keys and turned to face him. "Thank you for saving my life. I'll never be able to repay you for it, but I want you to know that I am well aware I would be dead if it weren't for you."

"Charlotte, you don't have to thank me. I -"

"But I can't be around you right now, Ren. You lied to me, and you did it for your own selfish reasons. The awful part is that if you had just told me the truth when Vince called, I would have stayed with you at the cabin for a while longer anyway."

He reached out to touch her, and she backed away, opening the door and stepping inside. "Please don't, Ren."

"Will you call me in a few days?"

"I don't know. I don't think so. I need to be alone right now."

"Charlotte -"

"Take care of yourself, okay?"

He nodded in defeat. "Be careful, please."

"I will. Goodbye, Ren."

She closed the door in his face. He waited a few minutes, his brain whirling and his stomach churning up bile.

*She needs more time. She'll realize that you did this because you loved her and –*

No. That wasn't going to happen. He had fucked up, and he needed to gather up what was left of his pride and let her go. He'd lost her forever, and he had no one to blame but himself.

* * *

"Look at you!" Charlotte clapped her hands when Darlene opened the door to the salon and slowly limped in. "No cane!"

Darlene made a short bow before limping her way to the reception desk. "It's about time. It's been over two months since the car accident."

Charlotte leaned against the desk. "Are you done with physio yet?"

"No. I've still got a few months of that." Darlene eased herself into the chair before turning on her computer. "How are you doing?"

"Fine." Charlotte smiled at her.

"Really?"

"Yes, really," Charlotte said as the bell over the door jingled, and Rita came sweeping in.

"Morning, ladies,"

"Morning," they replied in unison.

"What's the schedule look like today?" Rita leaned over Darlene's shoulder and peered at the screen. "Ugh, Mrs.

Munz is coming in. That woman drives me crazy. Her hair is so fried from those wretched perms she keeps making me do, but she insists that our hair product is doing it. Why she keeps coming back here, I'll never know."

Charlotte grinned as she walked to her station. "It's our sparkling personalities, Rita."

"Yes, that must be it," the older woman said. "But if -"

She stopped as the door opened, and a man entered the salon.

"Good morning," Darlene said. "How can we help you?"

"I'm wondering if I can get a haircut. I'm afraid I don't have an appointment."

"That's fine. We do walk-ins as well." Darlene pointed to the coat tree. "You can hang your jacket there, and we have coffee or tea if you'd like."

"No, thank you." The man hung up his suit jacket as Charlotte studied him. He was short with thick blond hair and dressed impeccably in a dark suit. His white shirt looked very bright against his tanned skin, and he straightened his tie as Darlene smiled at her.

"This is Charlotte. She'll be cutting your hair today."

"Hello, Charlotte. I'm Gareth." The man held out his hand, and she shook it before leading him to her station. He sat down, and she smiled at him.

"How much would you like taken off?"

He stared at her in the mirror. "Just a trim today, thank you."

"Sure. Come to the back, and we'll give it a quick wash first."

\* \* \*

"So, I've just moved to the area and wondered what to do for fun here?"

Charlotte paused with her scissors in her hand. Gareth had kept up a steady stream of chatter while she had washed his hair and started cutting it. She was only half-listening, and she smiled apologetically. "I'm sorry?"

"Just wondered if a pretty girl like you knew what people did for fun around here?" Gareth's smile was warm, but trickles of disquiet were zipping up and down her spine.

The man was handsome enough, but something about him made her nervous. She didn't know if it was because of the warmth in his voice and his smile not reaching his eyes or if it was the tattoos she could see on the back of his neck and through the sleeves of his thin shirt.

*Don't be ridiculous. Are you really going to judge someone because of tattoos? Ren has multiple tattoos, and he's the kindest, gentlest –*

She shut down her inner voice immediately. It had been over a month, and Ren had respected her wishes and hadn't tried to contact her. Of course, that didn't mean she didn't think about him way more than she should have.

The problem was that she wasn't thinking about how he lied to her but how much she missed him. As the days passed, her anger over his deception was fading more and more, and she had to stop herself from calling or texting him. Ren had crossed the line, and did she want a relationship with a man who tried to control her like that?

*Don't be an idiot. He did it because he loved you and wanted to give you more time to recover, not because he was trying to control you.*

That might have been partially true, but she wasn't stupid. His biggest reason for keeping her there was to try and convince her that she loved him too and –

*You do love him. So, what's the big deal? You're miserable without him, and it isn't just the sex you're missing. You really are stupid if you think that's all it is.*

"Charlotte?"

She forced herself to smile at the man sitting in the chair. "Sorry. I'm afraid I don't get out much, so I'm the wrong person to ask about entertainment options."

"I find that hard to believe. A gorgeous woman like yourself must have men knocking down your door to go out with them." Gareth's grin widened, and an odd trickle of fear went down Charlotte's back.

"Oh, you bet I do," she said. "My boyfriend's getting tired of replacing the door."

She didn't know why she lied, but the fine hairs on the back of her neck had stood up, and she white-knuckled the scissors in her hand.

"A boyfriend. What a shame," Gareth said.

She didn't reply and returned to cutting his hair as his gaze shifted to Darlene sitting at the reception desk. "What about you, pretty lady? What do you do for fun?"

Darlene grinned at him before patting her leg. "I've got a bum leg at the moment, so not much, I'm afraid."

"What did you do to your leg, Darlene?" Gareth said.

"Car accident a couple of months ago," she said. "It's doing much better now, though."

"I'm glad to hear it." Gareth watched as Rita swept up the hair around Charlotte's station. His eyes widened. "Is this… this is the salon that had that trouble with the motorcycle club last year, isn't it?"

"Yes," Darlene said with a glance at Charlotte.

"It's a miracle you all survived," Gareth said.

"We didn't." Rita's gaze drifted to Helen's station.

"Of course, I'm sorry. I forgot about what happened afterwards. I remember seeing on the news the story about how the prisoner sent hitmen after the entire salon," Gareth said.

Using a razor, Charlotte began to shave the back of his

neck. Gareth raised his voice over the hum. "You must have been relieved when he was killed in prison."

"You seem to know a lot about it," Charlotte said.

He shrugged. "It was all over the news. I suppose you wouldn't have known that, seeing as you were all tucked away in a safe house."

"That's right." She used a brush to sweep away the tiny hairs on the back of his neck. "All finished."

She took off the cape and shook it briskly as Gareth stood and studied his reflection. He ran a hand through his hair before grinning at Charlotte. "Best haircut I've ever had."

"Good. Thanks for coming by." Charlotte busied herself with tidying up as Gareth paid Darlene. He left the salon without saying anything else, and the small knot of tension in her belly loosened a little when the door shut behind him.

"Charlotte? What's wrong?" Darlene said.

"That guy just gave me the creeps." Charlotte popped her scissors and comb into the jar of disinfectant. "It's probably just me overreacting."

Darlene shrugged. "He seemed okay to me."

"Yeah, I guess. Although," Charlotte paused, "how did he know your name?"

"I must have mentioned it to him when he first came in." Darlene shrugged again.

"I don't remember that," Charlotte said.

"Maybe one of you said it." Darlene stood and limped to the back of the salon.

* * *

"Charlotte?"

Charlotte turned and smiled at Mel. "Mel! What are you doing here?"

Mel walked up the porch steps and held up the cups of steaming coffee she carried. "I brought coffee."

"You're a sweetheart. Come on in." Charlotte opened the door, and Mel followed her as she set her purse on the side table. She slipped off her shoes and handed one coffee to Charlotte as they walked to the living room.

"Were you at the gun range?"

Charlotte nodded as she sat on the couch and curled her legs under her. "I was."

"How do you find it?"

Charlotte shrugged and toyed with the lid of her coffee cup. "It's getting better. I don't know if I'd ever actually be able to use it against someone, but it's oddly comforting to know how to use a gun."

Mel sat at the other end of the couch and sipped her coffee as Charlotte glanced at her. "Were you just in the neighbourhood and decided to drop by?"

"Sort of." Mel hesitated and then gave Charlotte a soft smile. "We miss you, honey. You've been avoiding us for the last month."

"I haven't," Charlotte said. "I've just been busy."

When Mel just looked at her, she sighed and stared at her cup of coffee. "I have been. I'm sorry."

"We miss you, and we're worried about you."

"You don't need to be worried about me. I'm doing fine."

"Are you? You've lost weight, and you've got dark circles under your eyes. You look like shit, Charlotte," Mel said.

Charlotte laughed. "Thanks, Mel."

"Are you angry with us? Is that why you've been avoiding us?"

"What? Of course not. I love you and Vince. You know that."

"We love you too. So why are you ignoring our calls?" Mel asked.

Charlotte picked at the lid of her coffee cup. "You're close to Ren, and I don't want to risk running into him at your place."

"We wouldn't do that to you, Charlotte. If you don't want to see Ren, we'll respect that," Mel said.

I know. I just… you know."

"No, I don't," Mel said. "I know Ren held back the information about Steve being dead, but I also know he did it because he was worried about you."

"Did he? Or did he do it because he was trying to keep me to himself, trying to – to force me to feel something for him that I don't," Charlotte said.

"That doesn't seem like the Ren I know," Mel said.

"He should have told me the truth."

"Yes, he should have and believe me when I say that a day hasn't gone by where he doesn't wish he had."

"How is he?" Charlotte said.

"He's miserable. Vince says he can hardly concentrate at work and is dangerously close to being forced to go on leave or be fired. He's trying to pretend that he's fine, but he looks worse than you do." Mel reached over and took Charlotte's hand. "He loves you, Charlotte."

"Did you come here to try and convince me to talk to him?" Charlotte said.

"Partially. Mostly, I came by because we miss you and want to see you, but a part of me hoped to convince you how much Ren needs you."

"I thought you wanted me to be with Michael," Charlotte said. "Vince said you thought Michael would be better for me than Ren."

"I used to, but that was until I saw how miserable Ren is without you and now, how miserable you are without him," Mel said. "It's killing the both of you to be apart."

"This is so fucked up," Charlotte groaned before rubbing her forehead. "I don't know what to think or do anymore."

"Do you love him?"

"I don't know. The guy has saved my life numerous times, and he's made no secret that he loves me, but I don't know if I love him. I just keep thinking about how we're so damn different, and I'm worried that, eventually, he'll get tired of me. Rick and I were so compatible, and I knew exactly what I was getting into with him. With Ren, there's this feeling of being out of control, and I – did you know that he killed a man in front of me?"

"I do," Mel said.

"The man was about to kill me, and Ren just broke his neck like it was nothing. I should be terrified of him, but all I can think about is how gentle and sweet he is with me. He could have hurt me that day in the salon, but he didn't. I had to practically force him to have sex with me."

Charlotte gave Mel a look of misery. "I feel so guilty, Mel. I slept with another man three months after I buried my husband, and," she held up her hand when Mel opened her mouth, "I know there were reasons for doing it, but I enjoyed it. I *wanted* it. At the cabin, we did nothing but fuck like goddamn bunnies, and I loved every minute of it. I like sleeping with Ren more than I liked sleeping with my husband. What kind of horrible person does that make me? How could I do that to Rick? How could I -"

Her throat closed, and the tears that were threatening burst free like water from a broken dam. Mel slid across the couch and put her arms around her. She rocked back and forth as Charlotte buried her face in the crook of Mel's neck and cried.

After a few minutes, she sat up and gave Mel a watery smile. "I'm sorry."

"Don't be." Mel handed her a tissue, and Charlotte wiped her eyes and blew her nose.

"Do you feel better?" Mel said.

"Yeah, a little."

"Honey, will you take my advice?" Mel said.

"Yes."

"I think you love Ren, and you're finding that difficult because of your guilt. But, honey, I know that Rick wants you to be happy. He doesn't want you living alone and mourning him for the rest of your life. If being with Ren makes you happy, I know Rick would be happy for you. You can't let your guilt keep you away from Ren. You and Ren are different, but you need to take a chance with him. You'll spend the rest of your life regretting it if you don't."

"I know. But it's difficult."

"I know it is," Mel said. "But from what I can see, living without Ren will be even more difficult. You need each other."

"I miss him," Charlotte said. "I miss him so much I can barely think straight."

"Then call him. Ask him to go for coffee," Mel said.

"Yeah, maybe I will." Charlotte hugged Mel hard. "Thank you."

"You're welcome, sweetie. Now, let's talk about what evening you're coming over for dinner."

# CHAPTER 15

Charlotte repeatedly sneezed before coughing. She groaned and peered blearily at the package of cold medicine in front of her. The day after her talk with Mel, she had come down with a bad cold, and after two days of sneezing and a horrible sinus headache, she'd finally admitted defeat and called in sick to work.

Clutching the cold medicine, she shuffled to the kitchen and turned on the tea kettle. Her head was pounding, and she grimaced at her reflection in the window. Her nose was swollen, and bright red, and her cheeks were bright with fever. She poured herself a glass of water and shook two of the colourful orange capsules into her hand. She would take some meds and go back to bed. Maybe then her headache would –

Her cell phone rang shrilly at her, and she winced and rubbed at her temples before picking up the phone and squinting at the screen. It was the number for the salon, and swallowing down her irritation, she answered it. "Hey, Darlene."

There was no reply, and she looked at her phone before holding it to her ear again. "Darlene? Are you there?"

"Charlotte?" Darlene's voice was so low she could barely hear her.

"Darlene? Can you speak up? I think we've got a bad connection."

"Charlotte, I – you need to come to the salon." Darlene cleared her throat.

"Darlene, I'm seriously sick over here. Can't you reschedule my -"

"No. I'm afraid she cannot." A male voice spoke replaced Darlene's, and tendrils of fear slithered down Charlotte's spine.

"Who is this?" she said.

"You don't remember me? That's a bit insulting," the man said. "I remember you, Charlotte."

"Who is this?" she repeated.

"Gareth. You cut my hair last week. We discussed what a person could do for entertainment in this pathetic little town. Do you remember me now?"

"Yes." Her throat tickled, and she ignored the urge to cough. "What do you want?"

"Here's the thing, Charlotte. I wasn't lying when I said I was new to town, but I *was* fibbing when I said I had moved here. I haven't actually moved here. I'm just in town to pick up my brother's ashes."

Charlotte squeezed her phone with fingers that had gone numb. "Your brother."

"Yes. My brother. Perhaps you'll remember him – his name was Steve."

Her breath rushed out of her lungs, and she swallowed compulsively as Gareth spoke again. "Are you still with me, Charlotte?"

"Y-yes," she said.

"Good. I need you to come by the salon. Darlene, Rita, and I have been having a wonderful time together, but I think it would be even better if you joined us. Don't you?"

"And if I don't?" she said.

"I'll kill Darlene and Rita. And Charlotte? It won't be quick. I'll make them suffer."

"I'm on my way," Charlotte said.

"Excellent. I expect you'll be a good girl and not call your friend Officer Shallen. Am I right?"

"Yes," she said.

"Good. Because if you call the police, if you tell anyone, I'll kill your two little girlfriends here without a second thought. Do you believe me?"

"Yes."

"That's my good girl. You have fifteen minutes before I start hurting Darlene. See you soon, sweetheart."

He ended the call, and Charlotte stared wide-eyed at her cell phone before running to her bedroom. She dressed hurriedly, cursing as she fumbled into her clothing and staring at the alarm clock as the minutes ticked.

She opened her closet and moved aside the suitcase before yanking the gun safe out of the closet. She took three deep breaths, holding her hands out until they had stopped shaking, and then punched in the code. The safe opened with a quiet click, and she pulled out the gun and quickly loaded it. She grabbed the ankle holster sitting in the bottom of the safe and strapped it around her leg before easing the weapon into the holster. She rolled the leg of her jeans down, hiding the holster, and bolted from the bedroom.

* * *

"You did the right thing calling me, Charlotte," Vince said. "Where are you?"

"I'm almost to the salon." Charlotte turned left and laid on the horn when a car slowed in front of her.

"What? Charlotte, do not go into that salon. Do you hear me?"

"I have to!" she said. "I've got four minutes before this Gareth hurts Darlene."

"Charlotte, do not go into that salon," Vince said. "We're sending a swat team right now and -"

"If he sees them, he'll kill all of us," Charlotte said. "You can't let him know you're there. Do you hear me?"

"Charlotte, don't -"

"I love you, Vince. I have to go." Charlotte ended the call and turned into the salon parking lot. She parked and ran to the door. The closed sign was hanging in the window, and the shade was drawn, and she used her key to open the door. She stepped into the salon, breathing a sigh of relief, when she saw Rita and Darlene huddled together at Rita's station. "Are you guys okay?"

Rita nodded as Gareth smiled at her from the reception desk. "Welcome to the party, Charlotte. Lock the door, please, and join your friends."

She locked the door and joined Rita and Darlene as Gareth stood and moved to the middle of the salon. He studied them silently, and Charlotte glanced at the gun in his right hand.

He smiled at her. "So, you're the bitch who got my brother killed."

"He got himself killed," she said.

Gareth laughed. "Yes, I suppose he did." He took a few steps closer. "My brother was an asshole."

Charlotte's mouth dropped in surprise, and Gareth shrugged. "He really was. We hated each other as children, and that hatred carried into adulthood. He was a weak idiot who couldn't keep his nose out of trouble. In and out of different prisons for most of his life, and then becoming the leader of that ridiculous motorcycle club."

He snorted and rolled his eyes. "My mother used to say that he was a good boy, that it was the drugs that turned him bad, but of course, she didn't see the way he used to torture our schoolmates. He was an asshole, even as a child. God, he drove me fucking crazy."

"Then why are you here?" Charlotte said. "If you hated him so much, why are you doing this?"

"He's still my brother, Charlotte. Family is family, no matter how foolish they are. What kind of man would I be if I didn't take my revenge on the people who killed him?"

"We didn't kill him," Charlotte said. "He made his choice, and it resulted in his death. How is that our fault?"

He waved his gun in an irritated manner. "Small details, Charlotte. Small details."

"So what? Now you're going to kill us?" Darlene whispered.

"Yes, I am, Darlene," he said.

Rita moaned in dismay, and Gareth grinned at her. "Don't worry. If you're good, I'll make it quick and painless."

He cocked his head and stared at Darlene. "Although, you certainly are a pretty little thing, aren't you? Maybe we should get to know each other a little better."

Darlene took a step back as Charlotte moved in front of her. "You're not touching her."

Gareth laughed. "Are you going to stop me? Or maybe you're volunteering to go in her place? After all, if I remember the court records correctly – you're more than willing to fuck someone you barely know."

Charlotte didn't reply, and Gareth grinned at her. "What do you say, Charlotte? Maybe you and I should go to the backroom and do a re-enactment. I'll confess, lovely Darlene is more to my taste, but I won't turn down a free fuck."

"I'm not going anywhere with you," Charlotte said. "If you're smart, you'll leave the salon right now."

There was a sharp rapping on the door, and Gareth's eyes widened with surprise. He raised his finger to his lips as the knocking came again.

"Charlotte? Are you in there? It's Ren. I need to talk to you. I know you're angry with me, but you can't keep avoiding me."

A smile crept across Gareth's face, and he pointed the gun at Darlene. "Let him in."

Fear turned Charlotte's blood ice cold. "No. You don't want him in here. He's a cop."

"Oh, I know exactly who he is, Charlotte. Detective Flynn stopping by to chat has just made my job much easier. Let him in."

Darlene limped to the door and turned the deadbolt as Gareth retreated to the reception desk. She opened the door, and Ren shouldered past her. "Darlene? Why is the salon closed in the middle of the day? Where's Charlotte? I need to speak to her."

His gaze landed on Charlotte, and he smiled tentatively at her. "Hi. I know you said you didn't want to see me, but -"

"Hello, Detective Flynn."

Ren turned and frowned at Gareth. "Who are you?"

"My name's Gareth. Gareth Terrence. Big brother to one Steve Terrence." He raised his hands from behind the desk and rested his gun on the shiny surface, his finger resting on the trigger.

Ren stiffened, and he glanced at Charlotte before turning back to Gareth. "Your brother is dead."

"I'm well aware of that, Detective Flynn," Gareth said. "Darlene, go and join Charlotte and Rita, please." He watched as Darlene limped back to the others before smiling at Ren.

"Now," he raised his gun and pointed it at Ren's face, "why

don't you take out your gun and put it on the floor. Nice and slowly, please."

Ren reached into his jacket and pulled his gun free of the holster. He set it on the floor, and Gareth nodded. "Excellent. The ankle one as well, please."

He hesitated, and Gareth scowled at him. "Quickly, Detective Flynn. Unless you'd like to see what Charlotte looks like with a bullet in her forehead?"

Ren knelt and removed the gun from around his calf before standing and backing away.

"Thank you." Gareth picked up both guns and set them on the desk before motioning to Charlotte. "Come here, please, Charlotte."

She squeezed Darlene's cold hand and joined Gareth. He moved behind her and put one hard arm around her waist before pointing the barrel of the gun against her abdomen. He kissed her cheek, smiling when Ren growled loudly, and rubbed her side.

"You have a fever, Charlotte."

She didn't reply, and he squeezed her tightly. "Are you sick?"

"I have a cold," she said.

"You do sound a bit nasally," he said. "Have you tried using one of those Neti pots? They work wonders."

"What is it that you want?" Ren said.

"Really? You haven't figured it out?" Gareth shook his head. "Don't cops have to pass an intelligence test to enter the police force? Jesus."

He kissed Charlotte's cheek again. "I want revenge, Detective Flynn. Like any good brother would."

"Let them go. I'm the one who got Steve killed," Ren said.

"You do have a point. You were, after all, directly responsible for sending Steve to prison. How did it feel to live with Steve's gang? Did you find it difficult? Steve wasn't the most even-tempered guy. Also, not very bright. After all, he let an undercover cop into the club."

He sighed. "I was just telling these lovely ladies what an idiot my brother was, but I suppose I don't have to tell you that. You lived with him."

"So, let them go, and you and I can talk this out – man to man," Ren said.

Gareth laughed. "Man to man? Oh please, Detective. You've been watching too many *Law and Order* reruns."

He stared thoughtfully at Ren. The large man's glance kept darting to Charlotte's face, and Gareth squeezed her waist. "I think the detective has a crush on you, Charlotte. You must have given him one hell of a ride that day in the salon. Did you? Did you fuck him until he was -"

"Shut your fucking face." Ren's hands clenched into fists, and he took a step forward.

"No, no, no," Gareth admonished before pointing the gun at Charlotte's head. "Unless you want to see her brains splattered all over the floor, you won't come any closer."

Ren stopped, and Charlotte swallowed hard at the fear in his eyes. He took a deep breath. "It'll be okay, honey."

"So sweet." Gareth rolled his eyes. "I can't figure out which of you I want to kill first."

Charlotte stiffened in his embrace, and Gareth grinned at her. "I was going to kill you first, but I've changed my mind. Say goodbye to your Detective Flynn, little Charlotte."

"No, wait!" Charlotte said as Gareth pointed his gun at Ren.

Without stopping to think about it, Ren was dead if she did, she stomped viciously on the top of Gareth's foot. He shouted in pain, and she drove her elbow into his flat abdomen as hard as she could. His shout turned into a harsh groan, and when his arm loosened, she yanked herself out of his grip and scrambled to the left as Ren darted forward and tackled Gareth.

The two men fell to the floor, the gun trapped between them, as Ren raised his fist and drove it toward Gareth's face. The smaller man blocked it with his left arm, grunting with effort and whipping his head to the right when Ren tried to headbutt him.

The gun went off with a deafening bang, and Darlene screamed shrilly as Ren stiffened. Gareth grinned and shoved Ren off of him and onto his back. Charlotte stared at Ren's leg as Gareth staggered to his feet. There was a spreading patch of blood on Ren's thigh, and Gareth grinned again as he raised the gun and pointed it at Ren's head.

"Say hello to my brother, Detective Flynn," Gareth said.

There was another loud bang, and Gareth jerked in surprise before staring at his chest. He brushed aside the jacket of his suit and touched the blood soaking into his white shirt gingerly.

"What?" he whispered.

He took a staggering step backward and then crumpled to the floor. The gun fell from his hand, and he sucked in a shuddering breath before the light faded from his eyes, and his body went still.

"Ren!" Charlotte tucked her gun back into the holster around her ankle before falling to her knees beside him. "Honey! Look at me!"

"Charlotte?" Ren said.

"You're going to be just fine, honey. Just lie still," she said.

Rita crouched next to her. "Charlotte, there's so much blood."

Charlotte glanced at Ren's leg. His jean-clad thigh was already soaked in blood, and she could see more blood pouring out of the bottom of his jeans to pool on the floor.

"Fuck!" Charlotte unbuckled Ren's belt and yanked it free

before wrapping it around his thigh and pulling it tight. He groaned as the belt bit into his leg, and she used her right hand to stroke his forehead.

"I'm sorry, honey. I know it hurts."

The salon's front door burst open, and Vince, wearing a bullet-proof vest, rushed in, followed by a team of men dressed in black combat gear and helmets.

"Ren? Ren, open your eyes." Charlotte slapped Ren on the face, and he groaned and blinked rapidly. His face was pale, and he couldn't focus on her. Fear rushed through her. "Ren! Stay with me!"

"Charlotte," he whispered.

She leaned down and placed her mouth at his ear. "I love you, Ren. Don't leave me. Do you hear me? I love you."

# CHAPTER 16

"How is he?" Mel hurried into the hospital's waiting room.

"He's still in surgery. He lost a lot of blood," Vince said.

"But he'll live, right?" Mel asked.

"I don't know," Vince said. "He lost so much blood."

Mel squeezed his shoulder and reached for Charlotte's hand, who was sitting next to Vince. "He'll be okay, honey."

She didn't reply. She stared at her hands stained red with Ren's blood. Mel sat down beside her and put her arm around her.

"What happened?" Mel said.

"This guy, Gareth, was Steve's brother. He wanted revenge for Steve's death, and he took over the salon," Vince said.

"He came in a week or so earlier." Charlotte didn't look up from her blood-stained hands. "I gave him a haircut, and even then, something about him made me nervous. I called in sick to work this morning, and then Gareth had Darlene call me. He told me not to call the police and to just come to the salon, but I called Vince on the way there."

"You did the right thing, sweetie," Mel said.

"Did I?" Charlotte raised her head. "Ren was shot. He could be dying."

She stared accusingly at Vince. "Why did you let him come into the salon?"

"I couldn't stop him," Vince said. "Once he found out you were there, he insisted."

"You should have stopped him," Charlotte said, anger making her body vibrate. "You shouldn't have let him anywhere near the salon. Gareth wanted revenge on all of us, and sending Ren in there was a death sentence for him."

"It was our best idea, Charlotte," Vince said. "If Gareth knew we were out there, he would have killed the three of you. Sending Ren in at least gave you a chance. Ren said he could distract him and overpower him."

"Is that what happened?" Mel said.

Charlotte laughed bitterly. "He distracted him by getting shot. Then I shot Gareth."

"Oh, sweetie." Mel hugged her, but Charlotte pulled away.

"I'm fine. I'd kill the bastard again if I could."

"Charlotte," Mel said.

"I mean it," Charlotte said. "If Ren dies…"

"He's not going to die." Mel rested her hand against Charlotte's forehead. "Honey, you're burning up. You need to go home and get some rest."

"It's just a cold," Charlotte said. "I'm not going anywhere."

"Charlotte -"

Mel stopped as a surgeon came into the waiting room. He pulled his cap from his head and smiled at Vince. "Officer Shallen?"

"Yes, how is he?" Vince said as the three of them stood.

"He made it through the surgery. There was quite a bit of damage done to the muscles, and the bullet cracked his femur, but he was quite lucky, considering the amount of blood loss. We gave him blood transfusions and repaired the damage to the muscles and the nerves. He should recover well with time."

"That's wonderful. Thank you so much," Vince said.

"Can I see him?" Charlotte said.

"Who are you?" the surgeon asked.

"I'm his girlfriend."

"Oh. You can see him, but you'll need to wait a bit longer. He's still in recovery, but you can visit with him as soon as he's transferred to the ICU. He won't likely wake until tomorrow, though. We'll be giving him quite a bit of pain relief, and it'll keep him knocked out."

"I don't care. I want to see him," Charlotte said.

"Right. Well, I'll send a nurse out once he's in the ICU." The surgeon shook Vince's hand, and then Charlotte's before leaving the waiting room.

"Charlotte, maybe you should go home and get some rest. If Ren's not going to wake up tonight, then -"

"No," Charlotte said. "I'm not leaving, Mel."

"All right." Mel smiled at her. "At least come to the cafeteria with me and get something to eat."

She took Charlotte's arm and tugged her toward the elevator.

\* \* \*

HE DRIFTED IN THE DARK, HIS THOUGHTS BLEARY AND HIS LEG throbbing dully. He shifted and groaned as pain shot through his thigh. A soft hand rested on his forehead, and joy flooded him when he heard her quiet voice.

"You're okay, honey. Try not to move."

He wanted to speak, but the dark wouldn't let him. His eyelids were incredibly heavy, and his entire body felt weak and disconnected from his brain. Charlotte's hand slipped into his, and he felt her warm lips press against his ear.

"Can you squeeze my hand, honey?"

He squeezed, and after a moment, she spoke again, "Just try once, Ren. Please, honey."

Frowning, he squeezed again, and she made a soft sound of relief. "That's good, love. Go back to sleep now."

* * *

"Happy to be home?" Vince asked as he pushed the wheelchair out of the elevator and down the hallway toward Ren's apartment.

"I'd be happier if I weren't in a wheelchair like a damn invalid," Ren said.

Vince grinned. "You can use the crutches around the apartment, but it's better to have the wheelchair for longer trips. At least for a while longer."

Vince opened the door to his apartment and pushed him down the hallway toward his bedroom. "Hey, at least you don't have any stairs to climb."

He pushed Ren up to the bed and helped him lie back. "How do you feel?"

"Okay," Ren gritted out.

"Yeah, sure you do." Vince disappeared into the bathroom and returned with a glass of water before handing him some pills. "Take these."

Ren swallowed the pills and collapsed against the pillow as Vince covered him with a blanket. "Get some sleep, okay?"

Ren nodded, and Vince patted his shoulder before leaving the bedroom. Ren stared at the ceiling. He had spent five days in the hospital, and he was ridiculously happy to be back in his own place. He pulled his phone from his pocket, wincing as pain threaded through his leg, and checked his text messages. There was nothing, and he sighed before tossing his cell onto the bedside table.

When he had woken after nearly two days in a drug-induced haze, Vince had been sitting next to his bed.

"Charlotte?" Ren rasped out. "Is she okay?"

"She's fine," Vince said. "Well, she had a nasty cold, but other than that, she's perfectly fine."

"Are you sure?"

"Yes. She's good," Vine said. "I promise you, Ren."

He spent the next three days hoping she would show up, but she hadn't. He refrained from asking Vince and Mel about her, resigning himself to the fact that Charlotte still didn't want anything to do with him. He wondered if the memory of Charlotte telling him to squeeze her hand had been nothing more than a drug-fueled fantasy. As the days passed and she didn't appear at the hospital, he convinced himself it was.

He closed his eyes. The drugs were doing their job, dulling the pain in his leg and making him sleepy, and he drifted.

* * *

HE WOKE A FEW HOURS LATER WITH HIS BLADDER THROBBING. He sat up, rubbing his hand across his forehead and looking for his crutches. Vince had left them propped up against the far wall, and there was no way in hell he could reach them.

He cleared his throat and called for Vince. "Vince? Hey, Vince, can you come here for a minute?"

He almost fell off the bed when the bedroom door opened, and Charlotte entered the room.

"What's wrong?" Her voice was husky with her cold, and her nose was red. She coughed into the crook of her arm before wiping her nose with a tissue.

159

He stared blankly at her, and she hurried to the side of the bed and rested her hand on his good leg. "Ren? Are you okay? Is your leg hurting?"

"No, I have to pee," he said stupidly.

"Do you want the crutches or the wheelchair?"

"Crutches."

"Okay. Let's get you sitting up on the side of the bed first." She helped him swing his legs over the side of the bed, frowning when he winced. "Are you all right?"

"Yes." He cleared his throat again. "Charlotte, what – what are you doing here?"

She smiled at him. "Vince had to leave."

She reached for the crutches and hesitated before reaching into her pocket. "Hold on." She pulled out a small bottle of hand sanitizer and quickly doused her hands in it. "The last thing you need is my cold."

She brought the crutches to him and helped him stand, grunting a little with the effort, and then slipped the crutches under his arms. "Okay?"

"Yeah." He moved awkwardly to the bathroom, and she followed him into the small room. He gave her an embarrassed look that she didn't seem to notice as she reached for the waistband of his track pants.

"Uh, I can do it," he said.

"Right, of course." Her face flushed, and she stepped out of the room.

When he finished, he crutched into his bedroom. Charlotte stood right outside the bathroom door, and she followed him back to the bed. He sat on the bed with a harsh grunt, and she placed the crutches against the wall before helping him ease his leg onto the bed.

She propped some pillows behind him, and he reclined with a soft sigh as she patted his good leg. "I've made some stew. Do you think you could eat some?"

"Yes." He searched her face as she smiled again at him.

"I'll be right back."

She returned five minutes later, carrying a tray with two bowls of stew and two glasses of water. She gave him a bowl, placing a glass of water on the bedside, before climbing onto the bed beside him. She spooned some stew into her mouth before frowning at him. "You're not eating."

He took a bite of the stew. It was delicious, and his stomach growled in response. After five days of hospital food, the stew was like a little piece of heaven. "It tastes delicious."

"Does it? I can't taste a thing." She smiled ruefully before coughing.

"Have you been to the doctor?"

She shook her head. "It's just a cold, Ren. I'm already feeling better than I did."

They finished eating in silence, and she took his empty bowl and set it on the floor beside the bed. She clasped her hands around her knees and studied him carefully. "Tired?"

"A little."

"You should probably lie down again. You need your rest," she said.

She started to slide off the bed, and he grabbed her hand. "Charlotte?"

"Yes?"

"What are you doing here?"

"I told you – Vince couldn't stay."

"Why are you helping me?"

"Why wouldn't I?" she said.

"Because you hate me? Because I lied to you and tried to keep you at the cabin until you fell in love with me?"

"That was pretty stupid of you," she said.

"I know, and I'm sorry," he said.

"I know you are," she said. "And I don't hate you."

"You do, and you should. I've been a real asshole."

She scooted forward and stroked his chest with her warm hand. He shuddered under her touch, and when she started to move back, he put his arm around her waist and pressed her body against his. He had missed her terribly the last month and couldn't resist touching her.

"When Vince told me what was going on, I nearly lost it," he said. "I was, well, I was freaking out, and if it hadn't been for Vince, I would have gone charging into the salon like a bull in a china shop and gotten you killed."

She made a soft, soothing noise, and he rested his chin against the top of her head. "I was terrified Gareth was going to kill you."

She wrapped her arm around his waist. "I was terrified he was going to kill you."

She tilted her head to look up at him. "I've been going to the gun range like you suggested. I didn't want to – I hated it at first – but I'm so glad I kept going. If I hadn't, you'd be dead."

She blinked back the tears as he stroked her back. "It's over now."

"Yeah," she said.

"Were you at the hospital?" he said.

She nodded. "Yes, the day you were shot, I stayed with you. But my cold was getting worse, and I was afraid I would give it to you, so I stayed away."

"Thank you for staying with me today. With everything I've done to you, I know it's the last thing you want to do."

She sat up and frowned at him. "Ren, it's been killing me to stay away from you. I've been worried sick about you and driving Vince and Mel crazy with my texts to see how you are."

She shook her head. "I probably shouldn't be here now. If

I give you my cold, I'll feel terrible, but I couldn't stand being away from you any longer."

He was missing something. Something vitally important but for the life of him, he couldn't figure it out. "Charlotte, you hate me."

"Stop saying that," she said. "I love you."

His pulse thundered in his ears. "What?"

"I said I love you. Don't you remember after you were shot? I told you not to leave me and that I loved you?"

"I don't remember that."

She blew her breath out in a relieved rush. "Oh, thank God. I mean, not thank God you don't remember, but you were acting so weird when you saw me, and I thought maybe you didn't love me anymore and -"

"I will always love you," he said. "Always, Charlotte."

"I love you too, Ren. I'm sorry that it took you nearly dying for me to realize it. I mean, I think I already knew that I loved you, but I was an idiot. I had so much guilt over loving you, over wanting you, that I kept telling myself you didn't mean anything to me. But when Gareth shot you, and you almost died, I couldn't deny it any longer. I love you, Ren."

"I love you too," he said. "So fucking much."

He bent his head to kiss her, and she shook her head. "Better not. I'll give you my cold."

"I don't care." He took her mouth with his, kissing her deeply as he held her head steady with one large hand.

"I've missed you," he breathed against her lips.

"I've missed you too. I'm sorry I was such an idiot."

"You weren't."

"I was." She pressed her mouth against his again.

They kissed hungrily, and he cupped her breast, running his thumb over her nipple until she moaned.

"Let me show you how much I missed you," he said.

She grinned and scooted away. "Not a chance, Ren. You need to heal, and I'm not risking you tearing open stitches or reinjuring your leg because we're having sex."

"I'm willing to risk it," he said.

"I'm not," she said. "No sex for at least a couple of weeks."

He groaned, and she patted his chest. "Don't worry. We'll more than make up for it once you're healed."

He laughed and hugged her. "Promise?"

"Yes. I might even give your neighbours an earful by screaming about what a stud you are."

He laughed again. "I love you, Charlotte."

"I love you too, Ren."


Keep reading for an excerpt of Elizabeth Kelly's novel, "Shameless".

# SHAMELESS EXCERPT

*Maddie*

My car dying was the final straw. As the engine sputtered, choked, and coughed, I steered it to the side of the dark, silent road, shut it off, and rested my forehead on the steering wheel. The hot tears slid down my cheeks, tears I had desperately held back for hours. I let loose with a primal scream of fury and despair that echoed in the quiet interior of my car.

I screamed until my voice was hoarse. Until the rage and sorrow and utter disbelief that had been crowding my chest finally dissipated enough for me to take my first deep breath in hours. Panting harshly, I banged my fist against the dead car's dashboard before reaching for my purse.

I didn't have my cell phone. Of course, I didn't have it. I'd left it at home, determined not to have anyone interrupt my night of seduction. I planned on making Jordan turn his off as well. I wanted the night to be perfect, and hearing his damn phone chirping every five minutes wasn't a part of the perfect night.

I sighed and wiped at the tears still flowing down my face. Crying wasn't going to help. I needed to get my fat ass out of this car and back to that bar I had passed a few miles back. I hadn't given it much thought at the time, just a quick glance at the garish neon sign blinking in the darkness as I drove past it. Now, it was my only chance.

If I had been thinking clearly, I might have decided to wait in my car. I might have taken my chance with the next person who drove down that deserted country road. But my mind was still reeling, and my heart was still breaking, and I wanted nothing more than to be back in my tiny, lonely house. I used to hate that house. I dreamed nightly that Jordan would invite me to live with him in his perfectly acceptable townhouse. But now I wanted my home with a desperation born of panic and a desire to pretend my entire world hadn't been blown apart around me.

I grabbed my purse and my keys and climbed out of the car. I slammed the door harder than I needed to before trudging down the road. It was cold, and I pulled my thin wrap tightly around my curvy body. I glanced at my shoes, cursing myself in my head. I'd be lucky if I could even walk back to the bar in the damn things. They were stilettos and excruciatingly uncomfortable to walk in. Of course, I had worn them tonight intending to be fucked in them, not walking in them.

I put my head down and walked faster, teetering a little on the damn heels before catching my balance. The cold wind knifed across my body. I wasn't dressed for the weather. I tugged at my too-short dress and tried to use the wrap to cover my bare arms completely.

It was pointless. The wrap was poor protection against the wind. I wished bitterly that I was wearing my usual yoga pants and cardigan. At least then, I'd be warmer.

Of course, one didn't seduce their fiancé in yoga pants

and a cardigan, did they? No, they seduced them with six-inch stilettos, stockings, barely-there underwear, and the quintessential little black dress.

At least, I had assumed one did. After walking in on what I did, obviously I was mistaken. Or maybe it wouldn't have even mattered. Jordan might have been alone, taken one look at my chubby body poured into this ridiculous dress, and rejected me like he had so often in the last six months. And why wouldn't he? He was handsome, with a perfect body and a metabolism that allowed him to eat whatever the fuck he wanted. My overly curvy body and my constant struggle to lose weight had often been an annoyance to him.

*It has nothing to do with you, Maddie. You know that, right? He lied to you. He hid his true self and strung you along for four fucking years. You're better off without him.*

A sob escaped my throat, and I wiped savagely at the fresh tears. I needed to forget Jordan and his lies and concentrate on getting home.

\* \* \*

If I hadn't been so cold, if my feet weren't blistered and bleeding, I would have kept right on walking past the bar. Bikes and nothing but bikes filled the parking lot, and the building appeared on its last legs. It looked rough and dangerous and everything I had avoided my entire life but if I didn't get out of the wind soon, I really was going to freeze to death.

My entire body trembling from the cold, I climbed the splintered wooden steps and stared at the giant of a man blocking the front door. He was bald with tattoos scattered across his skull, and he looked me up and down as I cleared my throat.

"Um, can I go in?" I asked.

The man grunted, and I squeaked in surprise when he reached out and touched my dark hair. He gave me another once-over before stepping aside and opening the door.

"Entertainment's here, boys!" he shouted. I stepped back when I heard the roars of approval coming from within the bar.

"Go on, girl. Ain't no point in being shy now." The man leered at me before grabbing my arm and nearly shoving me into the bar.

I stumbled in my heels, reaching out and grabbing onto the nearest table in a desperate attempt to keep from falling flat on my face. I breathed a sigh of relief at the warmth of the bar. I was anxious to find the ladies' room to remove my shoes and rub some warmth back into my frozen toes. If I were lucky, maybe they'd have some Band-Aids I could slap on my bleeding blisters.

I glanced up, my face paling at the sight before me. The place didn't look like a typical bar. It had a long, curved bar with a mirror behind it and rows and rows of liquor bottles, and there were a few pool tables scattered about, but there were only a few tables, and most of the seats were torn, sagging couches and dirty overstuffed armchairs. But it wasn't the décor that made my blood run cold. Besides the bartender, the entire place was filled with men and only men. They were all big, tattooed, and absolutely dangerous looking, and every single one of them was staring at me like I was a glass of water and they were dying of thirst. I took a lurching step backward.

"I'm sorry. I – I think I'm in the wrong place."

I turned to flee. I didn't care how cold I was or how much further I had to walk. I had made a terrible mistake coming to this place.

"Where do you think you're going, pretty little bitch?" A man snagged my arm, pulling me to a stop.

He squeezed my arm as I stared up at him. He had long blond hair tied back in a ponytail and was built like a truck. He studied me briefly before his face broke out into a wide grin.

"Only one tonight, boys, but I reckon she's got enough meat on her bones to handle us. Don't you?" he shouted.

The men in the room laughed, and I pulled against his grip. "I'm sorry. This was a mistake, I don't -"

"Shut up," the man said. "We ain't paying you to talk."

He yanked my wrap away before reaching for my large breasts. Without stopping to consider the consequences, I slapped him as hard as I could across his face.

His head rocked back, and he stared at me in surprise before touching the blood on his lip. "You'll pay for that, you stupid bitch."

He raised his arm, and I cringed back. Before he could slap me, a hand caught his arm and yanked him away.

"Back the fuck off, Jenkins. She belongs to me."

"The fuck she does, Riley," Jenkins said.

"The fuck she doesn't," Riley said.

I stared numbly at the man standing next to Jenkins. He was a mountain of a man, and even though I was over six feet in my heels, I still felt short next to him. He wore jeans and a tight blue T-shirt. A black leather vest clung to his broad shoulders, and tattoos covered his thick neck. His dark hair was cut short, and my eyes lingered on the scar that was visible on his left temple. His nose had obviously been broken a few times. He pushed Jenkins back before taking my arm and yanking me into his embrace.

I had a quick, fleeting glance at his dark blue eyes before his mouth claimed mine. He shoved his tongue into my mouth as his hands gripped my ass, and he pressed my pelvis into his.

He was incredibly warm, and my frozen body instinctively pressed into him, seeking out his heat like a bee to a flower. As his tongue licked and stroked mine, I was shocked to hear my soft moan and even more surprised at the flicker of lust that lit in my belly. In all of my twenty-eight years, I had never once been kissed like this. I had never been so utterly and completely owned by a man's mouth, and my hands clutched at his broad shoulders as I returned his kiss shamelessly.

He curved his tongue under my upper lip and sucked hard on it, eliciting another soft moan before he tore his mouth from mine. I stared dazedly at him, not entirely willing to believe that it was his erection I was feeling against the curve of my belly. He gave me a warning look before sighing loudly.

"I told you not to drop by tonight, Kitten." There was an edge to his voice as he squeezed my waist, his fingers digging into my flesh. I knew instinctively that this man and his claim that I belonged to him was the only thing that would save me tonight.

"I'm sorry, baby," I said. "My car broke down, and I didn't know where else to go."

He sighed again, a *Can you believe the shit I have to deal with?* sigh, before turning to face the others. He kept his arm around me, pressing me tight against him as he waved his hand at the men in the bar. "Boys, this is Kitten. Kitten, these are the boys."

The men stared silently at me, and I licked my wind-chapped lips. "It's nice to meet you."

One of the older men with a long dark beard shot through with streaks of grey bellowed laughter. "There ain't no way in hell this pretty little filly would ever be seen with your ugly mug, Rye."

Riley scowled at him. "What the fuck is that supposed to mean?"

"He's sayin' you're ugly, boy." Jenkins clapped him on the back before giving me a once-over. "And this bitch ain't your type."

"How the fuck would you know what my type is?" Riley raised his eyebrows at him. "And stop looking at her like that, or I'll rip your fucking eyeballs out of your head. Got it?"

"Jaysus, boy." Jenkins gave him an exaggerated look of hurt. "Cool your jets. I didn't know she was your woman. Fuck, you never talk about her."

"Maybe because I didn't want you fucking leering at her like the goddamn pervert you are." Riley took my hand and led me toward the door. "C'mon, Kitten."

"Where do you think you're going?" A short man with a large beer belly and long white hair stood from one of the couches.

"I'm gonna take my woman home, and then I'll be back," Riley said.

"We got business to take care of," the man said.

"Yeah, I know. I won't be long."

The man shook his head. "She can stay."

"Frank, she doesn't need to -"

"I said she can stay. Unless," Frank cocked his head at Riley, "she don't know how to keep her mouth shut. Do you trust your little *kitten*, Riley?"

I started to tremble. Riley had stiffened against me, and there was something in how Frank looked at him that made my stomach churn.

"I trust her," Riley replied.

"Then there ain't a problem with her staying," Frank said.

Without speaking, Riley led me toward one of the dirty, worn armchairs. He sat down and pulled me roughly into his lap, pressing me back against his chest. My dress had ridden up until the tops of my stockings were showing. He rested his hand on my thigh, his fingers stroking the thin band of flesh that was peeking out from above the stocking.

I pulled on the bottom of my dress, trying to tug it down, and he grunted with disapproval before pushing my hand away. "Don't, Kitten."

The rest of the men were ignoring us now. A few of them had returned to playing pool while the others were conversing in small groups. Only Frank was still staring at us. I gave him a nervous look as Riley slipped his other hand under my long, dark hair and held the back of my neck in a firm grip.

He continued to stroke my smooth thigh, and I pushed down the new bite of lust. I was in deep trouble, and now was not the time for my libido to rear its ugly head.

"I have to use the bathroom," I whispered.

He pushed me to my feet and led me toward the back of the bar. I followed him meekly, my hand gripping his. I staggered a little when he led me down a dark hallway. He glanced back at me, his eyes unreadable in the dim light, before opening a door on the left.

"You have two minutes."

I hurried into the bathroom. I realized with surprise that I really did have to pee, and I eyed the dirty toilet with distaste before layering the top with toilet paper. I peed quickly, sighing with relief as my bladder emptied, then flushed the toilet and lurched my way to the mirror. I gripped the sink and stared at my reflection. My face, always pale to begin with, was deathly white, and my bright red lipstick was smeared.

I turned on the tap and used the water to wash my hands and scrub the remains of my lipstick from my lips and face. My hands were shaking badly, and my feet were screaming at me.

There was a small stool in the corner of the room, and I

limped my way to it before sitting down and slipping off my shoes. My feet practically shrieked *hallelujah,* and with a small groan, I massaged them gently. I was just inspecting the blood-soaked blister on the back of my right heel when the bathroom door banged open, and Riley walked in.

I shrank back as he slammed the door shut and squatted before me. He held my chin in a firm grip. "Who are you?"

"N-no one," I whispered.

"What are you doing at this bar?"

"I told you – my car broke down, and I just wanted to use a phone to call a tow truck, that's all. Please, let me go. You can slip me out the back or something, okay?" I pleaded.

"There isn't another place around for miles. You'll freeze to death."

"I'll walk back to my car and stay there until morning. Someone will come by, and I'll use their phone," I said.

He gave me a grim look. "The only people who will drive by are the men out there. Do you want them stopping to help you?"

I shook my head and blinked back the tears as Riley rubbed at his forehead. "Fuck. What's your name?"

"Maddie."

"Listen up, Maddie. The only way you'll survive this night is by doing everything I tell you to. Understand?"

I was so scared my throat had gone bone dry, and I couldn't squeak out a reply. He squeezed my chin. "The men out there are brutal and dangerous. If they think you're not who I say you are, they'll rape you, beat you, and leave you for dead. Do you understand?"

"Y-yes," I said.

"I can't let you leave out the back. If I do that, they'll beat the shit out of me and then find you and hurt you. Your only chance - *our* only chance - is to keep pretending that you belong to me."

"Why are you doing this?" I asked.

He hesitated before glancing at the bathroom floor. "You remind me of someone. Someone sweet and innocent who I failed to protect. And I'll be damned if it happens again."

"Who?" I said.

He frowned at me. "What?"

"Who do I remind you of?"

"It doesn't matter. Just keep your mouth shut and do whatever I tell you. Do you understand?"

"Yes."

He studied me carefully, and alarm flooded my nervous system when his eyes dropped to my large breasts. My dress was ridiculously low cut, and he got more than an eyeful of my cleavage.

"Christ," he suddenly muttered. He forced his gaze to my face, and my thighs trembled at the look of pure need on his face. I stared at his mouth, those full lips that had touched my own and made me forget that I was in a room full of dangerous, terrifying men.

*Don't be ridiculous, Maddie. Someone like him would not find someone like you attractive.*

No, he definitely wouldn't. Even though he wasn't conventionally attractive, something about him called to me. I had no trouble believing he could easily have whatever woman he wanted. His body was pure muscle, and the scar on his face only made him more mysterious and attractive.

It was absolutely the wrong moment for my lust to come roaring back to life, but apparently, I had zero control over it. I wanted him to kiss me again. I wanted to feel his hands on my breasts and his cock in my pussy while he whispered dirty things in my ear and –

"Fuck, Kitten. You've got your need written all over that pretty little face of yours," he groaned.

I jerked in surprise when he dropped to his knees in front

of me and yanked me forward. His crotch pressed against me, and my eyes widened when I felt the hard evidence of his arousal.

"Wha- what are you doing?" I squeaked.

"Giving you what you want," he growled.

# ABOUT THE AUTHOR

Elizabeth Kelly was born and raised in Ontario, Canada. She moved west as a teenager and now lives in Alberta with her husband and a menagerie of pets. She firmly believes that a person can survive solely on sushi and coffee, and only her husband's mad cooking skills prevents her from proving that theory.

For more information about Elizabeth, check out her website at

www.elizabethkelly.ca

facebook.com/EKellyBooks
instagram.com/elizabethkelly_author
amazon.com/Elizabeth-Kelly/e/B00EOHZ0MS
bookbub.com/authors/elizabeth-kelly

## ALSO BY ELIZABETH KELLY

**Tempted Series**

Tempted

Twice Tempted

Forever Tempted

Breathless

Tempted Trilogy (Books 1-3)

**Red Moon Series**

Red Moon

Red Moon Rising

Dark Moon

Alpha Moon

Pale Moon

**The Recruit Series**

The Recruit (Book One)

The Recruit (Book Two)

The Recruit (Book Three)

The Recruit (Book Four)

The Recruit (Book Five)

The Recruit (Book Six)

**The Shifters Series**

Willow and the Wolf (Book One)

Ava and the Bear (Book Two)

Katarina and the Bird (Book Three)

Porter's Mate (Book Four)

Bria and the Tiger (Book Five)

Rosalie Undone (Book Six)

The Dragon's Mate (Book Seven)

Rise of the Jaguar (Book Eight)

The Assassin and the Bear (Book Nine)

Elora and the Crow (Book Ten)

**The Draax Series**

Reign (Book One)

Rule (Book Two)

Rebel (Book Three)

Surrender (Book Four)

Survive (Book Five)

Salvation (Book Six)

**Harmony Falls Series**

Sweet Harmony (Book One)

Perfect Harmony (Book Two)

Forbidden Harmony (Book Three)

Redeeming Harmony (Book Four)

Absolute Harmony (Novella)

Beautiful Harmony (Book Five)

Reckless Harmony (Book Six)

**Seasoned Romance Series**

Bet Your Heart on Me (Book One)

Take a Chance on Me (Book Two)

Place Your Trust in Me (Book Three)

## Individual Books

The Necessary Engagement

Amelia's Touch

The Rancher's Daughter

Healing Gabriel

The Contract

A Home for Lily

Saving Charlotte

Shameless

The Fairy Tales Collection

Broken

An Unlikely Seduction

## Holiday Romance

The Christmas Wife

The Christmas Rescue

The Christmas Nanny

The Christmas Boss

Sordid Games